DON'T DROP THE POTATO

GEOFFREY C. PARKS

Palmetto Publishing Group
Charleston, SC

Don't Drop The Potato
Copyright © 2018 by Geoffrey C. Parks

First Edition

Printed in the United States

ISBN-13: 978-1-64111-268-0
ISBN-10: 1-64111-268-9

ACKNOWLEDGMENTS

To my wife, for whom I patiently wait to arise each morning so that I can read her my new pages. To my daughter, who is a gift from God and listens like no other. To my son, who's creative passion is limitless. To Dr. Marguerite Fairweather and the late Dr. Paul Fairweather, whose unconditional love and support saved my wretched life. To my dear friends and clients, who listen daily to my pages--it is the fuel that keeps me writing. To my copyeditor, Judi Heidel who sifted through my pages with an eagle's eye, never distorting my essence. To Bobby Yousefi, for my cover art, and my handsome grandson, who posed for the picture.

Finally, to every author I have ever read who has shared their heart with me. Blessed are those that come before us to light the way.

This is the first book in a trilogy.

Other Books by Geoffery Parks:
Ascension - can be purchased on Amazon or
Barnes and Noble

ARIZONA AND BACK

The smog alert warned people not to go outside, but there I am, sitting on a step in front of our shitty one-bedroom apartment, in a rundown neighborhood in Glendale, California, waiting for my dad's brother to pick us up and thinking to myself, there's got to be more to life than this. My dad's in jail again, and we don't have money to pay the rent or buy food because my mom is a manic-depressive crazy person who can't keep a job. Oh yeah, I'm Charles Becker, but my friends call me Chip. Nice to meet ya. I'm sixteen and pretty fuckin' lost. I won't realize how lost until about ten years from now when my acting coach tells me I've got anger issues and I should see a therapist. But I'll open that Pandora's box at a later time. Right now, I want to focus on the summer and fall of 1961 and all the crazy shit that happened to me.

The sound of a bicycle bell snapped me out of my zone. Suzi White, a cute red-headed girl, was cruising by on her bike wearing a pretty pink dress and waving at me. I don't know why anyone would ride a bike in a dress; it doesn't seem practical. It was hiked up pretty far, and her white legs glistened in the morning light. Suzi had been hanging out with my friend Jack, and he'd confided in me about her. He told me she was on her period, but as soon as she was off it they were gonna have sex.

I'd only kissed a girl once, well technically twice, and that was back on the East Coast when I was in the seventh grade. Her name was Cheryl Rigatano, a bouncy Italian girl, who was always laughing. We were jitterbug dance partners and used to go to classes together at the Girls Club every Friday after school. We competed in dance competitions and even got second place once. She won a pretty heart necklace, and I won a pair of gold-plated cuff links. She loved the necklace. I thought the gold-plated cuff links were a dumb prize for a thirteen-year-old kid, but I remember feeling proud when I walked up to the judges and they handed me the small velvet box.

One day after class, our student teacher, a plain girl with a face full of zits, told us she had something special to show us. We followed her out back to a quiet place be-hind the club, where she pulled out two pieces of paper and handed one to each of us. It was a kissing license. How she knew about a kissing license was beyond me, because at that time I didn't even know there was such a thing. Who knows why people come up with weird shit like that? Maybe it was all bullshit, and it was just a way for her to kiss cute boys. Anyway, she said she would demonstrate on me first, then I could try it with Cheryl. I just stood there like a dumbass as she stuck her tongue in my mouth and wiggled it around. It was a real shocker, but I liked it. When it was my turn to try it with Cheryl, it wasn't quite the same. She didn't open her mouth hardly at all, and she didn't wiggle her tongue. We never tried it again after that. My mom found the license in my pocket and beat me with a belt, her usual weapon for punishment. She told me I was a pervert, and I was never allowed to go back to the Girls Club again.

I watched Suzi disappear around the corner on her bike just as a big powder- blue four-door Oldsmobile came into view. I could see the guy behind the wheel craning his neck around and checking out the numbers on the apartments as he got closer. I saw the Arizona plates and figured it was my uncle Al. I sat there picking at a hole on the knee of my worn-out blue jeans, acting like I didn't see him. He pulled up right in front and honked. I didn't expect the honk, so I jumped a little and looked up. He nodded at me. I nodded back and he stepped out into the street. He was a tall, lean, muscular man, and I remember my dad telling me he fought in the middle-weight class. My dad was an amateur boxer, but Al fought pro, and I guess he had a pretty good record from what my dad said. He always told me Al had a long reach, which gave him an advantage in his weight class.

My mind flashed back to my first boxing match at the boys' club. I remember seeing the notice on the bulletin board: Boxing in the Gym: 4:00 p.m. I had never really boxed before, except one time when my little brother and I put on some big sixteen- ounce gloves that somebody had left lyin' around, and I pounded the crap out of him. The little shit would never quit. Even when he was crying, he would charge at me, swinging blindly. My dad had taught me to keep my left up and jab, and when I saw an opening, to let my opponent have it with my right.

I ended up in the ring with a tall, skinny black kid. The coach told us the rules and sent us to our corners. He blew a whistle, and I walked toward the black kid with my left hand up. He came at me like a whirling dervish, flailing his arms and smashing me to the floor. The whistle blew, and the coach came over to me as I struggled to get to my feet. He looked into my eyes and asked if I was okay. I nodded and we went back at it. Left hand up, jab, wait for an opening, then let my right fly. It never happened; he pounded me with overhand punches that sent me flat on my back. Everything was a blur. I could hear the coach yelling, "Stand back." When I came to my senses, the coach said, "That's it." I stumbled through the ropes and some kid helped take my gloves off and kept saying how I got my ass kicked. I told him to shut up, and I finished taking my gloves off myself. Then I went outside and waited for that son of a bitch. I had had a few street fights prior to this, and I always won. It was mostly wrestling, so I figured if I could get that tall fucker on the ground, I could beat him. But he never showed, or I was waiting in the wrong place. When I look back on it now, I was lucky he didn't show because he probably would have kicked my ass in the street too.

I was definitely not going to share this story with my uncle Al. As I watched him saunter toward me, I wondered if he remembered which brother I was because we hadn't seen each other for at least ten years. I stood up as tall as I could to greet him. He stuck out his hand and I shook it—he had a goddamn vice grip. He looked me right in the eye and said, "Hi, Charlie." I damn near broke down and started crying. His brown eyes looked just like my dad's. I said, "Hi," back, in a voice that didn't sound quite like my own. It meant a lot to me that he remembered my name. I wish I would have told him that, but hell, I was only sixteen and didn't talk about my feelings to anybody. I liked him immediately, and oddly enough, I felt safe around him. My brother moved up behind me and Al said, "How ya doin', Red?" My brother was a shy kid, so he smiled a little and backed away. I was always envious of my brother's red hair because it seemed to get him a lot of attention. I was what they called a dirty blond. I never liked that term; it made me feel like shit. My mom and uncle Al had their awkward greeting, and before you could count to ten, we had our three worn suitcases packed in the big ass trunk of the Olds. I sat in the front, and not much was said for a couple of hours till Al asked if anybody was hungry. I shrugged and said, "Sure." My brother mumbled something, but my mom didn't let out a peep. She was doing her proud thing. We did the drive-through at McDonalds and loaded up on burgers and fries and topped it off with a couple of chocolate shakes. We just sat in the car and ate. McDonalds was relatively new at the time, and I tell you, those were some of the best damn burgers I had ever eaten. Mom managed to make a face to let me know she thought the food was shit. After we all stuffed ourselves, Al suggested we use the restroom because he was gonna try to drive straight through to Tucson. The bathrooms were some of the cleanest I'd ever been in and are still damn good to this day.

We had only been driving a short while, when I noticed my brother had dozed off, and so had my mom, or maybe she was faking it because she didn't want to talk. Al started asking me some questions about school, sports, girls, and what I liked to do for fun. I told him I worked at a horse stable shoveling horse crap and brushing horses and the owner, Sam, a big-bellied wrangler, would let me ride for free. I told him Sam did stunts in the movies and was pretty well-known until one day he had a serious accident. He was doing a stunt in a Western where he gets shot and has to hang off the side of the horse with his foot in the stirrup. But the horse spooked and bucked, and his foot pulled out of the stirrup. He dropped like a sack of potatoes on his neck and broke it. He couldn't do stunts anymore and got a big settlement from the insurance company and that's how he got the money to open his stable. My uncle said he felt bad for Sam, but at least he got to be around horses. Uncle Al had a fondness for animals and told me he had Greyhound dogs that he trained and raced at the track and would take me there sometime if I liked. It was easy talking to him because he seemed interested in what I had to say. He never mentioned my dad once, and I was glad about that because I didn't really know how I felt, other than ashamed. I loved my dad and wished he didn't do dumb shit and get thrown in jail. I missed him.

I heard my uncle Al say, "We're here," as we pulled into the driveway of a single-story house. I guess I had dozed off. It was a nice house with a little front yard filled with cactus plants. My uncle Al told me they owned it and I could tell he was proud of that. We never owned a home or even lived in one place for very long. I'm not sure why, other than maybe my mom was try-ing to find some place happy where my dad didn't get in trouble and get thrown in jail. But that never happened, at least for the thirty years they were together. They had issues, but back then they called them problems.

It was getting dark, and a porch light came on as my aunt Dottie stepped through the front door and walked toward us. She was a big woman but moved with effortless grace. I found out later she had been a dancer most of her life, and during that first conversation she asked if I was still tap dancing. It amazed me she remembered that about me, but I guess it makes sense. If dancing is your life, you remember shit like that.

When we lived in New York, which is where I spent the first fourteen years of my life, I took tap for a year or so. I loved the sound of a room full of tappers doing their thing, even though my friends and brother made fun of me. They would follow me up the stairs to the dance studio and throw pebbles and razz me. I didn't give a shit because the teacher, Miss Sparling, was an ex-Rockette and probably the first woman I loved. She wore black fishnet nylons with a black leotard and had coal-black hair, which she always wore pulled back tight off her face. She also always wore bright red lipstick. But the most amazing thing about her was her grey-blue eyes. They reminded me of wolf eyes, and when she looked at me, I felt like what a rabbit must feel like right before a wolf devours it. I was the only boy in a room of about thirty girls. I felt awkward at first, but once I got focused on the "shuffle ball change," I got lost in the sound of those taps slappin' that wood floor and was swept up in the synchronicity of sound. Because I was the only boy, I got big parts in the performances we did, even though I wasn't that good. I remember one show in particular, "Hernando's Hideaway," where I wore all black with a red cummerbund. I tapped out on the stage, all alone, smiling ear to ear, which is what you had to do when you were performing. The number was a solo. I think I even sang, but for sure I said OIe, at the end, with a flourish of my arm above my head. I was only about eight years old, and I might have been scared. I don't remember. But what I do remember is how my body was so full of energy that I felt like I was floating across the floor. Being eight, I hadn't had sex or even masturbated yet, but as I reflect on that night, it was right up there with those kinds of feelings. I felt special.

My aunt Dottie gave me a big hug, and it's funny how small I felt in her arms. I could see my mother roll her eyes as my aunt Dottie gave my little brother the same treatment, and I'll be damned if she didn't greet my mother in the same way. My cousin Harry was a big, kind of soft-looking kid, but he had a handshake like his dad's, and something told me he was pretty tough. My cousin Elizabeth seemed sweet and shy. She wore big coke-bottle glasses that made her eyeballs seem huge, and when she took them off to rub her eye, I noticed one eye veered off to the side. That's probably why she was shy and didn't talk much. I felt bad for her. I never understood why some people were born with defects. Maybe to make us appreciate what we were born with? Couldn't God figure out another way?

My aunt had some ham sandwiches on the kitchen table, and a glass of milk for each of us. She offered my mom coffee, but Mom acted all demure, stating it would keep her up. Aunt Dottie said, "How about a cup of tea?" My mom made the weirdest face. She twisted her mouth and squinted her eyes at aunt Dottie. Then she said, "No," like she was the fucking queen of Sheba. It was one of my mom's crazy moments when she would make you feel less than her. I could tell my aunt's feelings were hurt. It was tense at the table, so I shoved the food down before something bad could happen. My aunt Dottie got up and did some dishes, and when we were finished, she hustled us into our bedroom. There was a nice bed with pretty covers on it and a couch all made up. That's where I was gonna sleep, on the couch, no matter what anyone said, and I did. Mom put our clothes in the dresser, and we said our awkward goodnights. I lay down on the couch and wondered how long this was gonna last.

I woke up to the smell of pancakes and bacon. My brother was still asleep. I don't know how he did it, but he always fell asleep before me and woke up after me. I guess that's how it is with a little brother; they feel safe so they can sleep better. Growing up, I don't think I ever felt safe, except maybe when my dad was around, but even then I was always worried about when he was gonna get thrown in jail again.

I pulled on my pants and walked out into the kitchen. Mom was sitting at the table drinking a cup of coffee with Dottie; Al was at the stove. Harry and Elizabeth were slumped on the couch looking bored and impatient. I guess they were having to wait for us to get up before they could eat breakfast. I was hungry as hell, so I went back into the bedroom and gave my brother a shove. He woke up slowly after a few more shoves, looking all dopey, and whined, "What?" "Breakfast, get your ass up," I said. I didn't leave it at that because he tended to fall back asleep. So, I pulled his ass outta bed and onto the floor. He struggled and whined a bunch more, but I knew he liked the attention.

I went directly to the table and took a seat next to my aunt Dottie. I sat up nice and straight and placed my hands on the table to let everyone know I was ready to eat. Harry and Elizabeth joined us, and my brother stumbled out, his red hair sticking up in all directions, making him look like he was nine instead of twelve. He was a cute little fucker, but a real pain in the ass at times. My uncle Al, still at the stove, bellowed, "Let's eat," in a raucous voice that sent a charge of energy through my body. I almost yelled out, "Fuck yeah!" but I didn't. One thing I remember loving about Sunday mornings was my dad making us pancakes and bacon. I couldn't help but wonder if Sunday morning pancakes were a family tradition. The pancakes were not quite as good as my dad's, but maybe that was because I was missing him, and maybe that made my taste buds do something weird. I watched my mom shovel in the pancakes and follow it up with gulps of coffee. I guess when you're hungry, you're not so demure.

Harry and Lizzy cleaned up the dishes. I helped a little because I had a plan to get out of the house and shoot some hoops in the school yard I had spotted across the street. I mentioned it to Harry, but he said I was nuts because it was hot as hell out there. It was only about ten thirty, and I thought he was just being a pussy, or that he wasn't very good and didn't want to embarrass himself. Right about then my uncle Al walked in and said, "What are you boys up to?" I threw Harry under the bus and said, "I was hoping Harry and me could go across the street and shoot some baskets, but he thinks it's too hot." "Well," he said, "he's right, but why don't you boys go and see if you can tough it out?" Harry moaned a bit, but he grabbed his ball and off we went.

When I stepped foot out the door of that air-conditioned house, I got blasted back to a childhood memory of me standing next to my dad in the basement of a three-story brownstone we lived in. My dad was the superintendent and he did all the maintenance in the building. He told me to stand back while he used an iron rod to open the door of the giant coal furnace. The big iron door would bang open, and a big whoosh of hot air would damn near knock me on my ass. The damn thing singed my eyebrows more than once. I always stood a little closer than my dad had told me to. I don't know why I didn't learn my lesson. I guess that's just my personality; I have to get my ass kicked a couple of times before I get the message. Or maybe I just like danger.

By the time we got to the basketball court, I realized what Harry was talking about. It was a hot fucker. I don't ever remember feeling heat like that in my life, even back East in the summer with all the humidity.

I don't know why people say "it's a dry heat" like it's a good thing. Give me the wet heat any day. I wasn't gonna admit how hot it was, so we shot a couple of games of horse. Harry was good and beat me the first game. He was ready to quit, but I said, "One more," so he cussed and said, "Okay." I won the second game, but by this time my feet were on fire. On the way back to the house, Harry and me got in an argument about frying an egg on the blacktop. He said, "No way would it fry an egg." I said, "I bet it will." And then we went at it. He told me I was ignorant and I told him he was a fat ass. By the time we got inside the house, we were both worked up and tramped into the kitchen and asked Aunt Dottie for an egg. She told us she was not going to waste food in that way and to stop bickering and go play Monopoly.

Lisa was all excited about this and set up the game on the living room floor, and all four of us kids dug into a game of Monopoly. Harry and I were still bickering but sat down to play, each of us with the idea of beating the other one. It's a pretty good game to kill time because, before I knew it, Aunt Dottie was telling us to wash up for dinner. Al had just walked in the front door and asked how everyone was doing. We all said, "Good." It's usually what kids say when adults ask that question, no matter how bad things are. Lisa ended up having the most houses and hotels, which was probably a good thing because it eased the tension between Harry and me. Aunt Dottie made fried chicken, mashed potatoes, and green beans. She was a damn good cook, not just because that was my favorite food to eat, but because however she cooked that chicken made you happy to be alive and sitting at that table.

The next couple of days were uneventful. Al would go to work before any of us kids woke up. Dottie would cook up some breakfast and we would just hang out. Then one morning, I woke up to my mom and Dottie arguing. Dottie's voice was firm and clear, but my mom was yelling hysterically. "How dare you accuse me of stealing? I'm a Marconi!" Marconi was my mother's maiden name, and she always used it as a reference to let people know how important she was, especially when she and my dad would get into it. She came from a big Italian family, six brothers and two sisters. I liked my aunts okay, but I only liked one of my uncles. He was labeled the odd duck in the family, and I guess that's why we got along so well. Birds of a feather and all that shit. He was my uncle Joe. My grandma had a cottage at the shore, in a little town called Westbrook, and sometimes my mom would take us to visit her. That's when I would see my uncle Joe. He loved the outdoors and nature. His stocky body was always suntanned, and he wore ragged shorts and a T-shirt with holes in it, and almost never wore shoes. He always had a floppy, dirty white hat perched on the top of his head and a stubby cigar, which was rarely lit, that he chewed on, and I just loved the smell of him. He would take me eel fishing at night on the sea wall, which was built to protect the beach-front houses from hurricane waters. If I hooked an eel on my drop line, I'd pull it in, and my uncle Joe would grab it with a towel, smack its head on the sea wall to knock it out, and throw it in a bucket of sea water. We wanted to keep them alive. He told me they were better bait that way. The next morning, we would hike to the estuary that ran behind an elementary school. We had to climb over a fence and walk through black mud and weeds to get to our secret spot. It felt like we were doing something illegal and I loved every minute of it. Joe would cut the squiggly eel up in chunks, and I would tie it to a drop line and toss it into the river. We had a ten-foot pole with a net at the end, and Joe would drop it into the water and hold it at the bottom. When I felt the drop line tugging, I would pull it in ever so slowly till it reached the net. I could see the crab chompin' down on the eel, and this is where things got tricky; this is where you could lose them. I would gently finesse the line high enough to get the crab over the metal edge of the net. It was important that they kept their mind on eating and didn't feel the change in upward movement. Once I got them over the edge and into the net, my uncle Joe would pull up on the pole, and the big blue crab would drop down into the netting, its claws snapping wildly and water spurting from its mouth. Uncle Joe would grab it by the pincers, or a certain spot on the back, so it couldn't nip him. Then he'd drop it into a metal bucket we brought with us. We did this for hours. Sometimes we would pull two up at the same time, and we would laugh like hell trying to get them out of the net and into the bucket, especially if one got loose and we had to chase it down through the black mud and weeds. My uncle Joe was a cool guy. There were rumors that he used to just take off and ride the rails all over the country. I for one believe it. Hell, one of my cousins even wrote a song about him.

The sound of Dottie's voice pulled me back to a reality I didn't want to face. She kept saying, "You just have to ask." But my mom wouldn't have it. She charged into the bedroom and told me to get my brother up and to get dressed. I knew it was no use arguing with her when she got this way, so I rousted him and we got dressed. Mom threw our clothes in the suitcases, grabbed my stupefied brother's hand, and hustled us out the front door. My aunt Dottie just stood at the door, dumbfounded, and watched. There was nothing she could do. Even if my uncle Al were there, he couldn't stop her; it was hopeless when she got like this. We banged out the front door and into the street. I didn't look back because I was too ashamed.

HITCHHIKING

We trudged across an open field, me lugging two of the bags while my mother labored with the other one as she dragged my dazed brother along by the arm. I don't know how she knew which highway to take; she was crazy, but she was smart. We stood on the side of the highway and stuck our thumbs out for a ride. We stood there for quite a while. It was already heating up, and here we were, three eggs getting ready to fry, when a tan station wagon with wood on the sides pulled over. The guy driving asked in a happy voice, "Need a lift?" I could feel the cool air from the air conditioning blowing through the open window. I nodded, and my mother and brother got in. I put the suitcases in the back seat and hopped in the front. He asked us if we were "headin' West like the old settlers." I was glad to see somebody was happy, because I sure as fuck wasn't. Mom said, "Glendale, California." I thought, for what? "I can get you part way there, folks," he said, and then he started in. He told us he was a salesman and that he had had a pretty darn good week so far, and he told us what his territory was. He went on and on talking about quotas, profit margins, and a big bonus. He sounded like he knew what he was talking about, but I was getting kind of bored as he rambled on. I thought I might even fall asleep. Then he told us he sold Hostess cupcakes. My head snapped forward and my eyes lit up like a goddamn Christmas tree when he mentioned that. He must have noticed my excitement because he told us to help ourselves to the samples he had in the back of the wagon. Mom grabbed a box and handed me up a couple. We ate as much as we wanted. He had it all: Ding Dongs, Ho-Hos, Sno Balls, Twinkies, and chocolate CupCakes, my personal favorite. I thought about being a cupcake salesman, driving around as free as a bird, and how, whenever you wanted, you could eat a cupcake or two. But then I thought this guy seemed lonely and not that happy, even though he put on a good show. It seemed like the most important thing in the world to him was his bonus. By the time he reached his turnoff, we had eaten ourselves sick. He pulled over to the side of the road and said, "Good luck, partner." I thanked him for the cupcakes, even though

I felt liked puking on his front seat because I had eaten so much.

We'd been trying to get a ride for hours when this beat-up car pulled past us at a snail's pace. Three bad-looking guys were in it. I was glad they passed us by, but a moment later I noticed they were pullin' a U-turn up the road a bit. My heart started to race. I didn't look at them, hoping they would just drive past, but they pulled up to us and stopped. One of the guys was an Albino with red eyes. The guy driving had teeth missing and tattoos on his neck and arms. I couldn't see the other guy too well. My body started pumping adrenalin, my jaw clenched, and I could hardly breathe. They were the scariest fuckers I had ever seen. My mind was blank, my mouth cotton. I was in some type of fear or shock; my instincts told me these guys were killers. I wasn't im-aging this; I knew it. No way was I getting in that car. They were talkin' shit to my mom, and she told them to get going and that we were waiting for someone. They laughed and mocked her, said some nasty shit to her that I've blocked out to this day, and finally pulled away. My heart was pounding; I felt like crying and bile came into my mouth. It was all I could do to keep from upchuck-ing those cupcakes. My head was spinning, and it took everything I had to keep from fainting. Moments like that you never forget. Those guys were devils. I watched the tail end of that piece of shit car till it disappeared in the distance. Fuck those guys. I was thankful my mom had told them to move on and that we were waiting for someone. That's what you call a good lie. Within a few minutes, another car pulled over. I was still reeling from my encounter with the devils when the driver of the car asked if we needed a lift. I looked at his face, his car, and said, "Yes, please." We got in and he drove off. He asked where we were heading. I said, "Glendale, California." He told us he could take us as far as El Centro. I nodded okay. We never said another word, none of us. I guess we were traumatized by those devils, and he must have sensed it somehow, because he just drove.

A few hours later, we found ourselves standing on the side of the road in the dusty town of El Centro. The darkness had settled in and everything seemed bleak. My mom walked us over to a shitty-looking motel and tried to get us a free room, but they said they didn't have any vacancies. That was bullshit because I had seen the vacancy sign out front. I was tired and hungry, but I didn't want to stay in that crappy place anyway; it probably had roaches and rats. Besides, I hated begging. Mom took us into a restaurant and told us to go into the bathroom and wash up. We pushed through the bathroom door and rushed to the urinal, unzipping our flies and pushing each other to see who was gonna go first. We both pulled out our dicks and started peeing at the same time. We were laughing and pissing everywhere, and I'm glad nobody walked in on us because they would have thought we were queer. It was a nasty bathroom, with dirty urinals and sinks, so what we did I don't think made it any worse. There were no paper towels and the hand soap smelled like cum. That's just a figure of speech because, for the life of me, I can't think of how to describe the smell of that stuff. So, the first thing to come into my mind was "cum," even though I'm not sure I knew what the smell of cum was. I guess I was just being gross. Anyway, we wiped our hands on each other and laughed our asses off. Brothers just fuck around like that; it's part of our DNA.

When we banged through the bathroom door, my mom was standing there looking pissed. She had that sixth sense where she could always tell when we were fucking around, even if she wasn't in the same room. Maybe she could tell because we were happy. Anyway, some people in the cafe were staring at us, so we headed out the door. My mom handed my brother and me a couple of packs of saltine crackers that she probably begged off the waitress. We ate them as we walked. I had no idea what my mom had in her mind, and I was too worn down to ask, so we just followed her. There were no street lights and just a sliver of a moon, so it was damn dark. I sensed my mom's step speed up a bit as she stepped off the road and onto some grass. We were all stumbling and falling on the uneven ground. My brother fell every ten feet, so I was telling him what a spaz he was and laughing, but my mom didn't think there was anything funny and would have smacked me, except I was out of range. She walked over to a bench and plopped the suitcase down. We were at the back of a small park lined with trees. She sat down. My brother sat next to her. I realized this was it, this was where we would spend the night. None of us said anything, and my brother fell asleep on my mom's lap. I watched my mom as her head slumped to one side. At first I thought she was thinking. Then her head slowly sank downward and rested on the top of the bench. She had fallen asleep. She looked small and I loved her. I sat there staring into the trees. An occasional car would go by, and every now and then a semitruck. But as the night droned on, silence permeated the park, and I was overwhelmed by a horrible sense of doom. I was dead tired, so tired I couldn't even feel how hungry I was. I started to cry, tears just poured down my face, but I was mad too. I wanted to blame somebody for my miserable life. Why did God do this? I tried to make sense of it, but as hard as I concentrated on it, I couldn't. I felt weak and small and sorry for myself and my shitty life. Then a strange calm took over my body, and that's when I realized there was no God and that if I was going to do anything, I would have to do it myself. I didn't need anybody. I didn't know what anything even meant. Maybe I was hallucinating, because the trees seemed to move in a weird, ghostly way. These were not the trees that give us life, but demon trees that bring fear and death. I'm sure there were other things that traumatized me during my childhood, like those devils earlier in the day, but this is one of those defining moments in my psyche that I'll probably take to the grave with me. I don't think I ever fell asleep. That night was a waking nightmare. I do know I was awake when the sun came up because I watched my mom lift her head and look around at our surroundings like she had no idea where we were. I hated her. She lifted my brother's head, and the poor little fucker looked like one of those starved kids in a

German concentration camp. He was always a skinny kid, partly because he was such a picky eater and partly genetics I guess.

We stumbled across the grass, which was loaded with gopher holes—the reason for our trouble the night before. I spotted a few of them checking us out, probably wondering who the assholes were caving in their holes. The suitcases seemed to weigh twice as much as they did yesterday, and my brother kept saying how hungry he was. I knew there wasn't any use in me complaining because, if I did, I would probably get smacked. The highway was empty in both directions. But before I could set the bags down, I saw a red car approaching in the distance. I stuck out my thumb and the '58, red Ford Fairlane pulled to a stop. I could hear Mexican rock music playing on the radio. I looked in and there was a Mexican guy with slicked back hair at the wheel. He said something in Spanish and smiled. I looked at my mom and brother and told them to get in. He said some more shit in Spanish and I told him Glendale, California. I figured he was asking where we were going. He said, "Los Angeles," and I said, "Si," since that was close enough and easier than trying to work out the details. The smell of fresh Naugahyde filled my nostrils. It was red and white tuck and roll leather. I found out later that guys would go down to Tijuana, Mexico to get cheap deals on tuck and roll upholstery. That's probably where he was coming from when he picked us up. He had a pair of fuzzy white dice hanging from his rearview mirror, and the gear shift knob was a chrome skull. This guy took pride in his ride. Suddenly I noticed him jerk his head back. I paid closer attention and realized he was nodding off. He started to doze off again and I shoved him. He woke up and stared at me. I didn't know if it pissed him off, but he made a motion like steering with his one hand, and I realized he was asking me to drive. My dad had let me drive a few times—never a stick shift—but I figured what the hell, better me drive than him fall asleep and run into a tree and kill us all. We switched seats and he helped me shift though the gears. It was a jerky start and I stalled it once, but soon we were cruising down the highway at about sixty miles an hour. He was asleep in seconds. My brother sat forward in the back seat, wide-eyed in awe of me, and my mom...I don't know what she thought. I was scared shitless, but I felt a sense of power behind the wheel of that hot rod Ford with the Mexican rock playing on the radio and its owner snoring in the background. I drove for a couple of hours and finally got the feel of how to keep the car in one lane. After a while, I even rested my left arm on the door, part way out the window, and drove with one hand. I think I was pretty much a natural. The Mexican guy finally woke up, looked over at me, and smiled. He was probably just happy to wake up alive. We changed places and it was my turn to knock out. I woke up when I felt the car slow down and bump into a driveway. I noticed a big sign with a picture of a lake and boats and Salton Sea written across the top, and another sign that said Bus Station. We all sat there for an awkward moment until the Mexican guy opened his door and said something in Spanish and motioned us to follow him. I jumped out of the Ford and my mom and little brother followed. He walked us into the bus station, went straight up to the counter, and bought three tickets to Los Angeles. He turned around and handed me the tickets and a twenty-dollar bill. I looked him in the eye and said, "Grashus." I guess the way I said it was weird because it made him laugh. He said, "De nada." I asked for his address to send him the money. Tears were welling up in my eyes by then, and I guess he understood because he said, "No," and turned and walked out of the bus station. I stood there for a moment till my little brother broke my trance by asking, "How much did he give ya?" "A lot," I told him.

I handed the twenty to my mom and we went to the cafe to get some food. We had two hours to kill before the bus arrived. It was no McDonald's, but the burgers and fries were decent. I guess I should have felt thankful, but I didn't. I couldn't stop thinking about what we would do when we got to LA. I watched my mom eating her burger. She had false teeth, and it was always a little strange to watch her eat. I imagined her teeth could fall out any minute. I laughed at the thought in spite of myself. Mom laughed with me in a goony way as she chomped her food. I wondered if she knew what I was thinking. She had a knack for that.

The bus arrived right on time. Thank God for that, because I had been playing tag with my brother and was getting bored, and when that happened we usually started pounding on each other, and he would start crying, and then my mother would take it out on me. My mother jumped up from her seat when she spotted the bus and said something about getting at the front of the line so we could all sit close to each other. My brother and I were still screwin' around when I felt her nails dig into my arm. I yanked it free and didn't let her know it hurt like hell. My mom pushed her way to the front of the line and we followed her onto the bus. Mom went directly to the back where a big bench seat stretched from one side to the other. We took the whole space for ourselves. I sat on the far end away from her and checked my arm. I didn't want her to see me looking at it because she would laugh at me and call me a sissy. My arm had four nasty puncture marks where she had dug her nails into me. Maybe I deserved it for not listening, but I really did hate her. The back seat was a good idea though, because we all fell asleep fast. I guess the night before was taking its toll on us.

HOME SWEET HOME

I had been awake for a while when the bus finally pulled to a stop in front of an old Spanish building that looked like something out of the movie *The Treasure of the Sierra Madre*. I liked that movie and the idea of a bunch of buddies finding gold. The fact that money can make a person do crazy shit, like kill a friend, scared me the first time I watched it, but then I thought that's why the world is so screwed up, because money is more important than friends. The funny thing is, it doesn't seem to matter if you have a lot of money or no money; it always seems to cause problems. It makes me think of the saying that was drilled into me in bible study: "It's easier for a camel to go through the eye of a needle than for a rich man to enter the kingdom of God." I always figured I'd rather be a rich man and try to squeeze through it. But after seeing that movie, I wasn't so sure.

Mom woke up, grabbed my brother, and hustled us off the bench and out the back door of the bus. The guy unloading the bags was moving slowly and my mom seemed very impatient. She managed to push her way to the front of the line of people waiting for their bags and got the guy to give us our bags first. People didn't like what she was doing because it was rude, but she didn't care. She scowled at them and yelled at me for not helping her. I felt embarrassed. You would think I might get used to it after a while, but I never did. Shame is a weird thing. Right up to this day, that feeling comes rushing in if I've made a mistake or done something silly where people look at me as if I'm strange or different.

We were rushing down the streets of Glendale, and the buildings started to look familiar. I wasn't sure what my mom had in mind, but she was definitely on a mission. She stopped abruptly in front of the welfare building and pulled my brother and me in close to her. Her breath was bad, but I didn't tell her because she was in one of those intense moods where you didn't fuck with her. She told us to look sad and tired and hungry. We both nodded and in we went. She didn't have to tell us to act that way; it was all true, especially the sad part. The only thing she left out was pissed off. We stood in line with a bunch of other losers and waited. This wasn't the first time I had done this, but I was older now and felt more resentful than ever about my shitty life. We were there for hours, and a good part of the time my brother and I sat on a bench while my mother talked to a lady with grey hair who kept looking over at us for some reason. We played our parts to a T, and if they were giving out Academy Awards for our performances, I would have won best actor and my brother would have won best supporting actor. Mom finally finished her business with the grey-haired lady and walked up to us with a look of great accomplishment on her face. She said, "Let's go."

We walked about ten blocks. Then I saw the red and white sign. We opened the door and walked into an open room with a long table in the center where a woman in a Salvation Army uniform was seated. She greeted us warmly and she and my mom talked quietly for a few minutes. I stood back with my little brother. I hated this shit. She took us into a dining room where people were seated around long tables eating dinner. My first thought was, I'm not eating. I hated begging. But when I saw the meatloaf and mashed potatoes, my stomach won out over my pride. We ate all we wanted. It was nowhere near what my aunt Dottie could do, but it filled my gut, and I was thankful. After dinner, we went into another room where some musicians were tuning their instruments. We sat in folding chairs with a bunch of other lost souls. They handed out pamphlets with lyrics on them and told us to join in if we felt the urge. When we were back East, I had played on a Salvation Army basketball team. I even banged the tambourine on a corner once during Christmas with a bunch of soldiers. But I was a lot younger then, and things like pride didn't matter that much. We sang lots of songs that night. My mom had a pretty voice and she looked happy, so I sang along with her and my brother and all the other poor slobs that didn't have a place to sleep or food to eat. Later in life, the only place I ever donated money to was the Salvation Army. So I guess in a way I'm paying them back. We finished the night with "He's Got the Whole World in His Hands." As I was singing it, every once in a while I would throw in a "bullshit." Not so anybody could hear, especially my mom, but loud enough so God could hear. Not that he's listening.

In the morning, we sat around the table eating oatmeal. There wasn't enough sugar in all the world to make that bowl of mush taste good. I never did like oatmeal, but this was some nasty shit. I tried to shove down as much as I could without puking, because who knew when our next meal was gonna be.

The welfare people had set us up with an apartment, so we hiked across town, lugging those shitty suitcases, trying to find where it was. We asked people along the way for directions, and we finally found the apartments, but ours was unit G, and we didn't see G anywhere. There was a driveway with three units on either side of it with garages in the back. A, B, C on one side and D, E, F on the other. It was a no frills kinda place, but it was clean looking, with a couple of potted plants here and there. I spotted a G on a unit above the garage to the left and my heart leapt. We hurried back to the bottom of the stairs where there was a mailbox that said G on it. Mom opened it and pulled out an envelope with the name Becker written across it. She tore it open and there were two keys inside: one for the mailbox and one for the apartment. We hiked up the wooden stairs and I felt kind of excited. Mom opened the door and we all pushed our way inside. There was a small kitchen on the left. In the living room there was a couch, a lamp, and a table; and in the bedroom there was a double bed and a dresser. Attached was a small bathroom with a shower. We had no blankets or sheets, and welfare didn't give us enough money for gas or electric, but it was a place to sleep. It's funny how such a simple thing as a place to sleep can make you feel hopeful.

Mom had gotten some food stamps from welfare, so we all walked to the little market about three blocks away. I knew the routine. Mom would get the bread and milk, and I would grab, bologna, cheese, and whatever else I could shove down my pants while she kept the person at the cash register distracted with small talk, which my mom had a real talent for. Standing in front of the refrigeration unit that held the cold cuts, I started to shake. I looked around to see if anybody was watching or if there were any overhead mirrors. It was a small market with nobody in it but us and the girl at the register. I clicked my teeth; it was a nervous habit I had right before I stole something. I wanted to run out of the store and never come back, but I knew my mom would be pissed if I did. I glanced down at the bologna, eyes back up to watch, my heart pounding. I grabbed a pack. Then I grabbed a pack of cheese and shoved them both down the front of my pants. I cringed at the cold plastic against my belly. I pulled my shirt down and made sure they were covered. I walked up next to Mom and smiled at the cashier, who was still blabblin' with my mom as she handed her the food stamps. I didn't breathe easy till we got home and Mom made us some bologna and cheese sandwiches with a glass of milk. The apartment was warm, so there was no need for covers that night, but sleeping on that old stained mattress was nasty. My mom put a couple of face towels down for our heads, and I recognized them from my aunt Dottie's house. She was a thief.

The next couple of weeks went by quick, except that I met these twin brothers, Bob and Bill, who lived around the corner. They were tough guys with what you would call anger issues today. Back then they were just badasses. I think it was because they were Seventh-Day Adventists and couldn't go out on Friday or Saturday night or have any booze, so they were all pent up. But that's just a theory; I'm no psychiatrist. We got along good, and they were always willing to share their food with me. The only thing is, their religion didn't allow them to eat meat. That alone would piss me off. Imagine never eating a burger. I don't think their parents liked me very much, but they weren't mean to me. The mom gave me a stack of clothes once; I guess she noticed I always wore pretty much the same stuff. Bob and Bill were a little heavier than me, but we were the same height, so they fit okay. There was this light pink shirt that had never been worn because neither Bob nor Bill wanted to have anything thing to do with it. They said it was queer. I liked it and didn't care if the shirt was queer because I wasn't. I thought it was a little weird, being Christians, that they felt so strongly about that. I guess growing up in a big city like New York, I wasn't as prejudiced as most people. Don't get me wrong; I'm no saint. I've talked shit about everybody. But I think that was just to make me feel better about myself. The truth is that, at that time in my life, I felt more like an outsider than any human being I had ever met. I had so much shame and guilt about myself and was so miserable with my shitty life that at times I wanted to kill myself.

SEX AND BETRAYAL

One day when my brother was sick, and I was bored out of my mind from being cooped up in the apartment, I took a walk around the neighborhood, and I'll be damned if I didn't run into Suzi White carrying a bag of groceries. She told me she was heading home and asked if I wanted to walk her. I said, "Sure." Sure is something I used to say when I didn't know what else to say. Sometimes it meant yes, sometimes it meant no, and sometimes I don't know what the hell it meant. She handed me her bag of groceries. The bag wasn't heavy at all, but I guess it was the polite thing to do, so I went along with it. I asked her how my friend Jack was because I hadn't seen him since I got back from Arizona. She told me they broke up. When we got to her house, she told me her parents were at work and I could come in if I wanted. My heart started racing. I was breathing heavy and I felt dizzy, which was weird because we had been walking slow. I said, "Sure." The inside of her house was nice; everything was very tidy and neat. She took the bag of groceries from me and told me she was gonna put the food in the fridge. I just stood there like a big, awkward dumbass and watched her as she walked toward the kitchen. I noticed she was wearing faded jean shorts that were ragged at the edges. She kicked off her pink sandals before she disappeared into the kitchen. I exhaled deeply. I guess I had been holding my breath for some reason. When she came out, she had unbuttoned her blouse so that I could see her white bra. Oh fuck, I thought. She took me over to the couch and we sat down together. I was scared but excited as hell. I didn't know what to do—kiss her, grab her tit, or stand on my fucking head. Thank God she was experienced. She told me to relax and asked if I had ever done it before. I wanted to lie, but I just mumbled, "No." She started kissing me and man could she wiggle her tongue. She stopped for a moment to take off her shirt and bra. She told me to take off my shirt, so I did. I reached out and touched her tit because I figured that's what I should do. She smiled, made a funny face, and moaned. She laid us back on the couch, me on top. My head was spinning. I was panting like a fucking dog as I gazed into her eyes. Her eyes were glassy and she had a strange look on her face. Then she pulled down her jean shorts and I saw her red pubic hair and I froze. She rubbed on me and told me to put it in. I tried to unbutton by pants, but I was having such a hard time she had to do it. She rubbed against me some more and moaned, "Put it in." I tried, but I couldn't get it to work. She took my penis in her hand and touched it to her vagina. I'm not sure if I ever got it in her because my body started to convulse in a way I had never experienced in my life. She held me to her and, after a few minutes, calmly got up and walked into the kitchen. I lay there feeling weird and wet. She came back with a glass of water, a spoon of sugar, and a towel. I was in a daze and thought I might cry. She wiped me off and told me to eat the sugar and drink the water, so I did. She told me it would get me hard faster so we could do it again. As I was finishing the water, there was a knock at the door. I jumped to my feet and grabbed my clothes. She led me into the kitchen where there was a small pantry and told me to hide in there. I pulled on my pants and shirt, squatted in a corner, and waited. I heard voices but couldn't make out what was being said. The voices stopped and I could hear the pat of feet coming toward me. The pantry door opened and it was Suzi, thank God. She told me it was my friend Jack and that he wanted to talk to me. My fucking heart started pounding and my whole body jerked in shock. How would he know I was here? Then it hit me; she had told him. I looked for a back door; I didn't want to face him. Suzi said, "He's waiting." Fuck you, I thought, fuck you. I walked out through the living room and out the front door. Jack was pacing up and down in front of the house. I still hadn't put my shoes on, and the concrete was scorching hot on my bare feet, but I didn't want to say, "Excuse me, I need to put my shoes on." So, I just let them burn. I figured it was good punishment for what I had done. We walked for a while in silence. Then he stopped abruptly and we faced each other. His face was bright red and all puffed up, and his eyes were bulging out of their sockets. His fists were clenched and I ex- pected a punch in the face at any moment. I could feel my face twitching and flinching as I waited for the blow. He asked me how it happened. I told him the whole rot- ten story, bit by bit, and I watched his fists open and close as he struggled with whether or not to punch me in the face. But he never swung. I told him he should hit me. I told him that a couple of times because I felt so bad and I thought it would make things better between us. When things cooled down, we both realized that it was her way of breaking up with him, because she was just too afraid to be honest. So, she was just mean. To be honest with another person about what you feel is the hardest thing we do. It was too hard for her to be honest with him about breaking up, hard for me to have done something I felt horrible about and not know how to fix, hard for him to get the news like this and to try to figure out who he wanted to punch. Fuck, I thought, I'm only sixteen and my life is a complicated goddamn mess. Maybe suicide isn't such a bad idea if I have to deal with shit like this for the rest of my life. After a while, we parted ways. I said goodbye to my friend and wondered if it would ever be the same after that day.

Years later, when I was out with some friends drinking, we pulled up in front of a party we were headed to and parked. As we were getting out of the car, Jack was standing at my door waiting for me to get out. When I stepped out, he blindsided me and knocked me on my ass. There was no warning. The whole rest of the night we all had fun and lots of laughs. I guess that old pain must have come up from deep inside his memory banks and took control of his brain. He didn't stop with the one punch either; he pounced on me and started to whale on me. I guess the survival thing kicked in, because I started to fight back and, in a flash, I had him in a headlock and was punching as hard as I could at his face. He yelled, "Okay, okay," and after a couple of more hits, I stopped. We just stood there and stared at each other and never said a word. Our friends were dumbfounded by the whole thing. It makes you realize what pent up feelings can do if you don't talk. Which none of us did.

HIGH SCHOOL

Summer ended and school started up. My brother was in junior high and it was my first year in high school. The twins' mom had given me enough clothes, so I didn't look like a homeless person, even though I still felt like one. I managed to figure out where my classrooms were, but I was always running to make it on time. I was behind in everything and didn't understand half the stuff I was being taught. I felt stupid, but I never mentioned it to the teachers because they didn't seem to care that much. There was one class I was good at: typing. I don't even know why I ended up in that class, but I liked it. I had decent speed and I rarely made a mistake. I liked the snapping sound of the keys; it was like I had dancing fingers. The teacher was a fragile-looking man and always wore bow ties. He didn't like me for some reason and made me sit at a desk right up in front of the class so he could keep an eye on me. I think he thought I was cheating. I don't know how you could cheat, because you had to turn your papers in every day. Maybe it was be-cause I barely got in under the bell, and he liked every-one to be there early to set their margins. Everything was timed, so I usually started a little behind all the other kids, and this upset him. I got an A in that class for my performance, but a U for unsatisfactory behavior. I think he should have gotten a U for being an unsatisfac-tory teacher.

A strange phenomenon occurred about my third day at school. Two of the prettiest girls in school glom-med on to me. They were senior cheerleaders, and for the life of me, I don't know why they did it. Maybe they just thought I looked so fucking lonely walking around that this was their way of doing a good deed. Whenever they spotted me, they would run up to me giggling and grab my arm, one on each side, and walk with me till they had to head to their class. Sometimes they had their cheerleader outfits on. Sharon was the team captain and seemed to get most of the attention from the boys. She had long black hair down to her butt and loved swinging it around, and I'm not talking about her hair. I thought Becca was prettier, maybe because she was more genu-ine. She was a nice person and treated me with respect. I might have even loved her, but she was way out of my league. What I remember most about her was her nose. She had the cutest button nose.

A couple of weeks into school, I ended up in a doctor's office. I remember having to pull my pants down as a doctor examined my penis and balls. I felt awkward standing there exposed and being looked at. I had never been circumcised, and I suspected my visit had something to do with that. After the exam, I sat in a chair while my mom talked to the doctor. Two days later I went back and a pretty nurse gave me a shot in my ass. I told her I didn't like needles, so she had me lie on a table while she did it. She was kind and gentle. I had no idea what the needle was for, but I was too embarrassed to ask because I thought it might be some defect I had. The following week I went back and was told to strip and put a blue gown on. I don't remember the details of the surgery because they put me out, but I came away from it without my foreskin. It hurt like hell for about a week and walking around school was a real problem. I couldn't run to my classes, so I was usually late and racked up a lot of tardy slips. My typing teacher made a point of asking why I was late and walking funny. It embarrassed me a lot because he did this in front of the whole class. I wanted to bash his face in, but I told him

I hurt my knee. It was the lie I told people when they asked what was wrong. Time passed and eventually I got used to how my penis looked. I went back for three or four more shots, and I finally got up the courage to ask the nurse why I was getting them. She told me one of my balls hadn't dropped down and the shot was to help facilitate the process. To this day, I'm not sure why my mom did all this or how she even knew about my problem, but I'm circumcised and I've got two normal balls.

One day, five weeks into the school year, I was standing in front of the candy store. It was a wooden shack located in an open courtyard of our school, and lots of kids hung out there. I was with the twins, sharing a candy bar, when I heard someone yell, "Hey, Becker!" It was Phil Bembrooke, a kid that bullied me all through junior high. He would sit behind me in math and stick me with pencils, or knock my books out of my hands in the hall, or come up behind me and slap me in the back of the head. I was scared of him and tried to avoid him whenever I could. But there was no avoiding him now. He came right up to me and gave me a shove. He was even bigger than he was the year before, and dumber looking. The twins looked at me to see what I was gonna do. Phil stood there with a dumbass grin on his face, like he was my friend, and this was just his way of saying hi in his fucked-up way. I don't know what came over me, but all the shit that had happened to me over the summer—the hitchhiking, the sex, my dad being in prison, having my dick cut on—came surging up from inside of me and I tore into that motherfucker with all the fury of a raging bull that had been prodded and stabbed a dozen times by a matador and had finally had enough. I had been in a few fights before, but it was more wrestling. This was the first time I ever bashed anybody in the face. He was on the ground in a flash, and I was on top pounding him. The twins were rooting me on until someone yelled "teacher," and Bill pulled me off, and we ran like hell while everyone scattered.

Sitting in my classroom, sucking the blood off my cut knuckles, rethinking my fight with Phil, I guessed that when I was trying to bash Phil's face in, I must have missed a couple of times and hit the ground. They were a mess. I caught sight of a kid walking in, and he handed a pink slip to the teacher. Pink slips usually meant someone was in trouble and was being summoned to the dean's office. When she called out my name, my heart sank. As I stood up, a murmur rippled through the classroom. I guess several of the kids had seen the fight. The teacher shushed the class as she looked at me with disdain and handed me the dreaded pink slip. Why pink, why not a black spot like in *Treasure Island,* where the pirate who receives it knows his wretched life is done for? The long walk to the dean's office gave me time to think. My first thought was to run, but my feet kept me going in the direction of the office. I decided I was going to tell Dean Bell all about how Phil tortured me last year, and even started it this year by shoving me, and how he deserved to have his ass kicked. But when I walked into the office and saw Phil sitting there blubbering about how I beat him up and saying that I didn't believe in God, an overwhelming feeling of guilt hammered me into the seat that Dean Bell told me to sit in. I mainly looked at Dean Bell, but occasionally I would catch a glimpse of Phil blubbering in his seat, holding up his broken glasses as proof how he had been brutalized. Dean Bell asked me what I had to say about it all. Not one word came out of my mouth. I just sat there till he had no choice but to expel me for two weeks. Plus, I ended up having to get a get a job in a laundry sweeping and mopping floors to pay for Phil's glasses. I never told my mom I got expelled from school. She would never understand why I beat the crap out of Phil. Besides, ever since I could remember, she would take anyone's side but mine, even if the other person were the devil himself.

During my special vacation, I made a new friend. His name was Steve Smith and he lived down the street from me. His mom was a full-blooded Blackfoot Indian. Steve never mentioned his dad; it was almost like he didn't have one. Not that he got defensive about it when I asked him. It was like some kind of Indian magic where his mother got pregnant and he just popped out on the floor of the teepee of his own accord. His mother was a big, scary woman with raven-black hair, chiseled features, and a giant beak of a nose. She never wore a bra, and she had huge tits with giant nipples that were always in your face. She was strict as hell and was constantly yelling at Steve about one thing or another. And she definitely didn't like my ass, no matter how nice I acted. She probably noticed me staring at her nipples, but damn it, it wasn't my fault she wasn't wearing a bra.

I found out that the Blackfoot Indians got their name from the black leather moccasins they wore. And after I got to know Steve, he told me his Indian name was Huritt, which meant handsome, and he was. The only thing was, he was kind of awkward. Back then we called kids like him a spaz. He tended to bang into shit or trip over stuff. I liked him a lot and thought he was funny, but most kids made fun of him, so he was pretty much a loner, except for me. We always met outside his house to avoid his mother's wrath, and during my expulsion from school we would hitchhike up to Frank's house, a friend of Steve's, who lived a few miles away. I don't know how Steve met him. He was a nice enough guy, but strange. He smoked like a chimney. We did too when we were with him, but we never had money to buy cigs, so Frank would always offer up his. He was a thin, fair-skinned guy with sandy-blond hair, and he had this permanent tremor in his hands that seemed to run through his whole body. Steve told me Frank had been in a mental hospital for a time, but this was never talked about. He was eighteen and not in school. He watched the news all day and was always cussing out Eisenhower and Kennedy for being pussies about something called the Bay of Pigs in Cuba. He said they were chickenshit for abandoning all those guys who had tried to get Fidel Castro out of power because he was a no-good commie bastard. He explained how the CIA trained these Cuban revolutionaries to get Castro out of power, but it was a shitstorm, and 118 men were killed and 1202 were captured and put in prison because we didn't give them the backup that we promised. How the fuck he remembered all this shit was beyond me. He would go on and on about the Russians getting the first commie bastard in space and even knew his name—Yuri Kielbasa, or some shit like that—I don't remember. The other thing was, he always combined commie and bastard together, like it was somebody's first and last name. It was all boring shit if you ask me, but both his parents worked during the day, so we would just hang out at his house all day and eat. His parents had two refrigerators, one in the house and one in the garage. The one in the garage was a freezer; I had never seen anything like it. It was packed full of all kinds of meat. Frank told us we could eat certain things that his parents didn't keep track of. It was fuckin' great. Frank was a vegetarian, the first one I had ever met, and one time I was messing with him while I was eating a burger, making mooing sounds and shit like that. That's the first time I saw him lose his shit. He smashed his fist on the table and told us to get the fuck out of his house. I couldn't even apologize because he was ranting and raving and waving his arms above his head. Steve grabbed me and pushed me out the front door. It reminded me of my mother when she would have one of her seizures. I knew when she got like that it was better to disappear. As far back as age three or four, I remember my mom fighting with my dad, and when she didn't get her way she would work herself into a frenzy—and then faint. My dad would catch her and lay her on the floor. Spittle would sputter out of her mouth, and her eyes would roll back in her head. It was an awful sight, and my dad would kneel next to her and lift her head up a bit. He would tell me to get a wet hand towel. His voice was rough, but I'm not sure what he really felt. Deep down, I felt like my mom was faking, but I followed orders and would bring my dad the wet towel. I watched him wipe the spittle from her lips and then place the towel on her forehead. Eventually she would come around. The whole thing sickened me, and not in a way that I felt sorry for her, but in a way that it made me hate her because I thought it was all a fake. I didn't talk to anyone about these feelings for years. I felt bad about teasing Frank and must have been super quiet, because on the way home Steve told me not to worry about it, that tomorrow he would forget the whole thing. That made sense to me. It's kind of how crazy people act.

THE SKATER

Steve was a roller skater and kept on me about it. He wanted me to go with him to the rink. One day he even said he would pay if I went with him. When I was a little kid, I had skated with my older sister a bunch of times. I was never very good; I just liked to go fast. But it had been a while and I really had no interest. Steve could be a pain in the ass when he set his mind on something, but I figured if he was gonna pay, he must really want me to go to see how good he was. So I said okay, and then Steve yelled, "We're goin'! It's friends skate free night." He had suckered me, but he was so damn excited I just went along.

We got to the Starlight Roller Rink at about seven o'clock and it was already hopping. Steve knew the guy at the window, so we didn't have to wait in line. I noticed a big yellow sign on the wall as we entered that read: No Roughhousing, No Profanity, No Exceptions. Fuck me, I thought. Steve had his own skates, but he rushed me over to the rental area to make sure I was taken care of. The organ music was playing and skaters were zooming off and on the rink in a wild whirlwind of excitement. Some girl bumped right into me and damn near knocked me on my ass. She was all sweaty and laughing like hell as she took off across the carpet, running from her stupid girlfriend. She never even said sorry. I remembered this about roller rinks from when I was a kid—people bumping into each other all over the place and most of them never saying sorry. I know I never did. Steve flirted with the girl behind the counter who was helping me with my skates. Her name tag said Heather on it. Steve told her to get me a nice pair or he wouldn't skate with her anymore. She put on a sad face and said, "I'll never skate again then," and both she and Steve giggled like a couple of goons. He was so excited he was busting out of his skin, so I told him to go ahead and get his skates on and get out there. That's all it took. He said, "See you out there," and ran to a bench to put on his skates.

He was gone by the time I got to the bench, and I could see him cutting in and out of people on the crowded floor with a smooth, rhythmic style. He was damn good. I got my skates all laced up and headed for the floor. There was carpet everywhere but the rink itself, so people couldn't go bashing into each other as much, which was a good thing because they would come flying off the rink onto the carpet and bang into each other like the stupid girl who banged into me. The only thing was, it made it difficult to get around. The better skaters made walking on the carpet look easy, but I damn near fell on my ass a few times. I made it onto the rink and that was even worse. I only got about twenty feet before my feet came out from under me, and I slammed into the floor on my hip, taking a little kid down with me. I looked at him. He gave me a dirty look, jumped to his feet, and took off. I never said, "Sorry."

It was scary down on the floor. Skaters zoomed past me on all sides, just missing me. I got up quick, but I was so disoriented that I lost my footing again and down I went. I yelled, "Fuck," then thought, oh shit, remembering the sign posted on the wall when we came in— No Exceptions. I think that's why nobody says sorry. They're all saying fuck you under their breath. When I looked up, Steve was standing over me and offered me his hand. I grabbed it and got to my feet. He looked me in the eyes and said, "Easy, just let the skates glide, let the skates do the work." I got going, and what he said helped me a lot. I started to remember the feeling from when I was a kid. Right glide, left glide, right glide…Before I knew it, I was cruisin' around that rink like a pro. Well, I wasn't falling on my ass every twenty feet. I got into the feel of it, crossing one skate in front of the other, and I even skated backwards a little. But that made me feel like a spaz, so I just stuck with going forward. Every so often, Steve would zoom by me, skating backwards and waving at me and smiling. Little by little I gained confidence, and soon I was cutting in and out around slower skaters. I must have been going pretty damn fast because one of the guys in a striped shirt blew his whistle at me and told me to slow down. Then the lights dimmed and Steve skated up next to me and said, "It's couples rexing, we have to get off." We skated off onto the carpet and stood next to the rail and waited. The announcer said, in a deep, singsong voice, "It's time for a little romance here at the Starlight Roller Rink. This dance is for couples only." Heather, the girl who helped me with my skates, came up to Steve and said, in a real tough voice, "I'll give you one more chance, but if you mess up we're done." And she gave him a girly shove. Steve smiled and looked at me and said, "Watch this." They skated out together, then moved up close to each other and started to skate backwards. Steve held his left arm across his chest, and Heather held her right hand across hers while they rested their palms against each other's lower back. They were all tangled up, but when the waltz came on, they moved like one person. It was pure magic. The rink was almost dark; tiny lights blinked overhead like stars and beams of light crisscrossed on the floor. There were couples of all ages gliding across the floor, but I gotta say, Steve and Heather were the best. It's amazing how someone can be such a spaz at so many things, but be as graceful as he was at skating. Steve even looked taller. The way he arched his torso, with his shoulders back, his head held high and proud, with his black hair swirling around his face, changed him. He looked to me like a handsome Indian chief with his beautiful Indian princess at his side. They raced like the wind through the crowd of other skaters with fluid ease, as if they were of another time and place. I couldn't take my eyes off them. The music, the beautiful dance moves they performed, took me back to my childhood days in the dance studio when the sound of tapping feet would fill my body with blissful energy. I could feel my eyes well up as I watched them because I knew Steve was in heaven.

THE PARTY

Hitching back from Frank's house one day, a young guy in a brand-new Volkswagen bus pulled over. It was a two-tone red and white, with whitewall tires and shiny moon hubcaps. We dashed for the bus. Steve beat me to the front door, and as we pushed and shoved at each other, the guy driving said it was a bench seat and we could both sit in front, so we did. The long gear shift was on the floor, and because I was squeezed in the middle, I had to move my leg over so the blond guy at the wheel could shift. Steve kept pushing me, and I kept pushing him, which made the guy driving laugh. He was asking questions like where were we going, what high school did we go to, shit like that. Steve and I kept fuckin' around and giggling like a couple of idiots, but we couldn't help ourselves; we were just feeling goofy. The guy asked us if we drank or ever smoked pot. This got our attention. Steve said, "Why are you a cop or somethin'?" The guy laughed and told us his name was Barry and that he wasn't a cop but thought we were fun and asked if we wanted to go to a cool party on Saturday night. He told us there would be free booze and pot. Something didn't seem right to me. This guy was like twenty-eight or something, and I wondered why he would invite a couple of goony teenagers to a cool party. Then it hit me; this guy thought Steve and I were queer. I was getting ready to say something, but the next thing out of his mouth was, "There will be lots of hot girls at the party." Before I could respond, Steve said, "How do we get there?" "I can pick you up if you want," Barry said. We were close to my apartment, so I told Barry to pull over. Steve said, "Okay," just as I elbowed him. He grunted. I was afraid Steve was gonna give Barry his address, so I said, "Pick us up right here." I pushed Steve out and shut the door behind me. Barry said, "I'll be here at nine. And wear something cool. It will be a blast." As he drove away, I told Steve what I thought. Steve shouted, "Bullshit," but I could tell he thought I might be right. We talked about it on the way home and decided that we should go because there would be free booze and pot and hot girls. I had never smoked pot and had only had a swig of Ten High Whiskey from a bottle at Frank's house. It tasted like shit, but sent a hot rush through my body that made me feel a little lightheaded and a little bit older.

I told my mom I was gonna spend the night at Steve's house. She liked Steve because "he had manners." I put on the pink shirt (it was the nicest shirt I owned) and my faded jeans. I loaded up my hair with Three Roses Butch Wax. I hadn't had a haircut for a while, but I managed to slick my top and sides back, and I thought it looked cool. I didn't have one pimple on my face, which was a fucking miracle because I had been plagued with them for the last few months.

I met Steve on the corner. He looked damn good. He was dressed in all black and had an Indian Bolo tie around his neck, with some sort of Indian figure hanging from the end. He told me it was a good luck thing. I asked him, "For what?" and he said, "To get laid." I said, "Fuck yeah." Steve told his mom he was spending the night at Frank's house, so we were ready to get crazy. Barry pulled up in the VW bus and we hopped in the front seat. He had Chubby Checker's "The Twist" blasting on the radio. He was twisting in his seat and taking a big drag off a joint. He passed it to me. Steve looked at me, I looked at him, then I took a big drag. I coughed it out before it got very far down my throat. Steve laughed, called me a pussy, grabbed the joint from my hand, and sucked in a big hit. He started coughing so hard that tears were running down his cheeks. I started poking him and punching him, and all the while I was laughing like a goddamn hyena. Barry let out a howl and peeled rubber down the street. He told us we were going to a bitchin' house in the Hollywood Hills. He said we might even see some celebrities there. We drove up a winding road, swaying to the music, and taking puffs off the joint. By the time we pulled up to the house, Steve and I were making weird faces at each other, sticking our tongues out, and just being goony.

There were lots of cars in front of the house and guys hanging out. The house was set back off the street and up some stairs. Fifty stairs to be exact; I counted them. The place was surrounded by trees and bushes. I had never been to a beautiful house like this before, and I felt a little out of place. Like somebody was gonna come up and tap me on the shoulder and say, "You're not supposed to be here." I still feel uneasy in fancy places, and I'm not sure if it's me or just the uptight vibe of proper behavior. I just don't like it. Everything felt a little weird and scary. Barry led us into the house and was saying hi to people and introducing us. Everybody was really nice, telling us their names and all. Like I was gonna remember. I wasn't sure what my own name was I was so high. Steve had this dumb, trancelike look on his face and wasn't talking at all. He just kept messing with the Indian Bolo that hung from his neck. Barry got us each a glass of brown booze and told us to drink it and that it would mellow us out a little. We must have looked uptight. I took a slug and so did Steve. It was hot going down my throat and into my gut. Oh, yeah, it was a rush.

We roamed around the house from room to room. "Hand Jive" was blasting on the stereo, and just about everyone was dancing, even in the backyard. The house overlooked the San Fernando Valley, and you could see the lights stretching out for miles. I stood in the backyard, tripping out on the lights for a long, long time, until some guy tapped me on my shoulder and asked me to dance. I realized I was dancing in place and moving my hands to the beat of the music. I was even singing the words out loud, like I was in the fucking shower or somethin'. I looked at the guy who was staring at me with wide eyes and a big smile. I laughed and said, "No thanks." I had never had a guy ask me to dance before. At least he didn't ask me to leave. I looked around, but I couldn't see Steve anywhere. Guys were dancing, drinking, smoking pot. It was a cool party, except I didn't see one girl. I saw a couple of guys making out on a lounge chair and thought, oh fuck. Some guy handed me a joint and said, "Have a toke mate?" He spoke with a strange accent. He had round wire-rimmed glassed on, and he was wearing a shiny sport jacket and tight-legged black pants. He told me his name was Todd and that he was from London. I took another swig of the brown poison in my glass and kept taking hits off the joint as Todd rambled on in his totally cool accent. He told me he thought my shirt was fab and that he loved my hair. The music was blaring and guys were dancing with each other, laughing, and having a great time. I was standing there in some sort of trance. A moment later, I was out in the center of the floor, dancing like a fucking half-crazed maniac with Todd and all those other guys. I was throwing my body around like a wild Indian, not caring who was watching or worrying if I would be asked to leave because I was too weird and didn't belong. I danced for hours and was sweating like a stuffed pig, so I tore off my shirt and tossed it in the air. A howl went up in the room and soon shirts were flying everywhere. I started howling and hooting along with everyone else. It was a tribal dance and it was fucking insane. I loved everybody and everybody loved me. It was the most fun I had ever had in my whole life.

I don't know how I ended up back in the VW bus, but there I was in the back seat, naked to the waste, with Todd leaning over me. I don't know if we kissed or not. My head was spinning, and I was falling in and out of consciousness when I heard Steve yell, "Get the fuck off him." Todd freaked out. Steve grabbed my arm, pulled me out of the van, and led me down the street away from the party. He had my shirt and helped me put it on. I was so fucked up I couldn't walk on my own, so Steve slung my arm over his shoulder as we made our way down out of the hills to a main street. Steve spotted a twenty-four-hour donut shop and we hobbled in. He sat me in a booth and ordered coffee and two glazed donuts. I gobbled up the donut and took swigs of the coffee. Steve was staring at me. I felt guilty, like I had done something wrong. I didn't know what had happened in that VW bus, but I was glad Steve pulled me out. I felt awkward sitting there. Steve said, "There were no girls, and you were right—he is queer; I should have listened to you." Then he said he was sorry and that he felt bad for getting us into that mess. We both agreed it was a cool party, except for the fact there were no hot girls.

But gay guys sure knew how to party. That's what Todd told me he was—gay. He said the word queer was out. Steve was messing with his Bolo tie. I nodded at it and said, "I guess that didn't work." Steve scowled at me and said, "Oh, it worked, it just wasn't the right sex." I spit the mouthful of coffee I had all over the table and both of us laughed like a couple of idiots. Sometimes, out of the blue, he said some really funny shit. We finished the coffee and made our way home. As I walked up the stairs to my apartment, I felt happy and sad, thinking Steve was a real friend.

HORSEBACK RIDING

I woke up in a fog, feeling afraid. My head hurt, and my mouth tasted like puke. My brother wasn't sleeping next to me; I had overslept. Sunday mornings my mom would take my brother to church. She had stopped trying to convince me I needed saving because I always put up such a fuss. It was weird to be in the apartment alone. I felt afraid, and I wanted to go back to sleep, but I had promised Bill I would take him to the stable to go riding. Bill had been bugging me for weeks to go riding, especially after I told him I would get him a cool horse to ride. The twins had done a lot for me, and I didn't want to let Bill down. I pushed myself out of bed, threw some water on my face, and brushed my teeth for twice as long as normal to get the puke taste out of my mouth. I didn't feel well at all. As I left the apartment and walked down the stairs, I started thinking about the nightmare that woke me up. In the nightmare, I was going to this house with a group of guys to put on a play or something. We were trying to find a place to rehearse. We walked past a woman of about twenty or so, who I think lived there. We found a quiet room and started to work on the show, or whatever it was we were performing. Some guys started to file in and sit in random chairs. It felt uncomfortable. Then this one asshole I had seen around before walked in and said some smartass thing to one of the guys I had come with. I told everyone we should leave because it was getting too crowded. The asshole was slouched on the couch next to another guy with a tattoo. The asshole said something I didn't quite hear, and I turned and told him to fuck off. He pulled out a gun and shot all my friends. Then I woke up. The dream or nightmare had left me with an uneasy feeling that I couldn't shake. I hurried up the front steps to Bill's house, and just as I was about to knock, the door opened. Bill was standing there with a paper bag in his hand and a disappointed look on his face. His mom stood right behind him. She acknowledged me with a nod and told Bill to have fun and to be careful. She put extra emphasis on the be careful part. He moved past me and down the steps. I stood there for a moment feeling that awkward feeling that only mothers can make you feel when they know you're gonna get in trouble before you even get in trouble. I said, "Sure," then chased after him. He was like a caged animal whose door had been opened, and he bolted through it to the call of the wild. He said he was pissed that I was so late. Before I could say sorry, he went into a rant about riding and told me he had ridden quite a few times, but not for a while, and that he had enough money for an hour. I told him I knew some cool trails, but we couldn't go that far in an hour. I didn't feel as excited as he did and told him I had gone to a party and had gotten shitfaced. I didn't give him any of details; Steve and I made a pact not to tell anyone about it, ever. He opened his paper bag and handed me a cucumber and cheese sandwich with the crust cut off. He didn't like the crust, so his mom always cut it off for him. I thought that was nice of her. She was a good mom, except for the Seventh-Day Adventist stuff, which the twins never stopped complaining about. I dug into the sandwich and immediately started to feel better.

Sundays at the stable were always busy, and when we got there it was hopping. The dandies were out in full force. A dandy was a word the wranglers gave to a person who acted and even dressed like they could ride, but didn't know the first thing about horses or how to sit a saddle. The beautiful smell of horse shit was in the air, and it made me happy. It's weird how the smell of shit can make you feel happy. I had told Sam we would be there, and as we walked up to him, I introduced him to Bill. He shook Bill's hand and gave us the royal treatment. He told me I could ride Cloud, a small paint horse that I liked to ride bareback. I always thought it was cool to ride without a saddle. He told me Bill could ride Sadie, one of the better stable horses. He also gave Bill an extra hour for free. It made me feel important that Sam would do that for me. He made his living off rentals, and I thanked him about twenty times. I told Bill to go pay at the window and to sign the release form so the stable wouldn't be responsible for any accident that might happen on the trail. I went to saddle up the horses, being sure to tell Bill that he couldn't come in the back where I was because it was only for staff. I felt important saying that, and he nodded okay. I greeted Cloud and rubbed her ear as I placed the bit in her mouth. She took it easily and I told her she was a good girl. Sadie was not as sweet. She was fine when I put the blanket on her, but when I threw the saddle on her, she got a bit skittish. I had to talk to her and calm her down. Then I eased the bit in her mouth, sweet-talking her all the time to get her to go along. Every horse has a different temperament. I learned that from Buck, an old leather-faced wrangler who was Sam's right-hand man. I think Buck was part horse what with the way he moved around them and the way they listened to him. I led the horses out of the barn to where Bill stood pacing excitedly. I told him to follow me. I led Sadie up to a wooden box with a step. It was where all the dandies who were renting mounted their horses. Bill stood there looking lost, so I told him to get up on the box. Sadie stood patiently as Bill mounted her. I checked his stirrups to make sure they were the right length. Bill watched me with a sense of awe as I adjusted the stirrups. I noticed he had a little different look on his face. He was still excited, but there was something else. Maybe he was a little nervous because he hadn't ridden for a while. I didn't use the box to mount Cloud. I stood next to her, grabbed a handful of mane, and swung my leg up and over her back. It was a clean mount. Sometimes I wouldn't make it all the way and would have to pull myself up, but this was a good mount. It made me feel good because a few of the dandies were watching me, and so was Bill. I felt like a real wrangler. I guided Cloud past Bill and gave him a nod to follow me. We made our way out of the stable and to the open trail. I watched how Bill handled Sadie. He seemed okay, but he wasn't as good as he told me he was; he didn't sit the saddle that well. He wanted to run the horses right away, but I told him to take it slow till we got across the bridge and down the trail a way. I had grown to respect horses during the six months I had worked at the stables and knew running them balls out wasn't the best thing to do. Sadie was a spirited horse, and I could tell Bill had his hands full trying to keep her at a walk. It felt good to be out in the fresh air on the trail, and as we rode past other riders, I felt strong and proud on my painted Indian pony. I held the reins in my right hand and let my left arm hang loosely at my side. I sort of slouched a little, which gave me the look of what I imagined an Indian warrior looked like on a casual ride. I looked down at my legs and at Cloud's hoofs as they hit the dirt trail and sent up little puffs of dust. I felt my body and I felt free. Bill trotted ahead a little and bounced in the saddle. I trotted up next to him. He asked again when we could run them. I told him we could canter as soon as we got around a bend in the trail up ahead because there was a straightaway, but we shouldn't go balls out. He nodded, and I could tell Sadie was ready to go. I noticed Bill bounced more as Sadie picked up her pace. When we rounded the bend, Sadie leapt forward, throwing Bill's shoulders back. I gave Cloud my heels and she lunged forward. I pulled up next to Bill, who was bouncing harder in his saddle. He was smiling, but there was another look in his eyes—one of uncertainty. I told him to rein Sadie in, but every time he would get some tension on the reins, he would bounce and lose the tension. Sadie was charging forward, and I was worried Bill couldn't hold her. Down the trail we flew, in a full gallop, growing dangerously close to the steep slope that led down into the LA River basin. I yelled at Bill to pull up, but he was out of control, bouncing up and down like a spastic rag doll. I urged Cloud on, and we tore down the trail trying to get in front of Bill, but Sadie was too damn fast and kept pulling away. Both horses were charging at a wild gallop. Sadie had that crazed look in her eyes, as if possessed by some primal demon, wanting to rid her mouth of the bit that controlled her animal spirit. Her head was lowered in a locked position so she could stop the pull on the bit. I had experienced that before, and the only way to break it was to pull on one rein more than the other while keeping tension on both to get the horse's head to turn a little, but Bill wasn't doing that. It was all I could do to rein in Cloud. I watched Bill disappear down the hill and out of sight. I slid to a stop at the top of the slope just in time to see Sadie veer off the trail and onto the steep cement wall of the wash. I held my breath and watched her fight desperately to hold her footing as her hoofs slipped wildly on the concrete—then she went down. It was a horrible sight as Bill bounced down the side of the cement wash, arms and legs flung in all directions till his body finally rolled to a stop. Sadie found her footing and charged off across the river basin and out of sight. I must have been in shock because I'm not sure what I did next. I think I ran down to look at Bill; his eyes were closed and he wasn't moving. There was blood on the cement under his head, and his arm was twisted behind his back. I ran back up and through a park toward some houses and pounded on the first door I came to. A white-haired woman answered, and I tried to explain to her what had happened and kept asking for her to call an ambulance or the police. I guess I was crying and hysterical because she kept telling me to calm down, and it would be okay, and that her husband would call for help. After he got off the phone, he told me to take him to where Bill was. The white-haired woman would wait at the house to show the ambulance where we were. As we trudged back through the park, the old man told me his name was Chuck. I had to keep slowing down and waiting for him because he was old and didn't move very fast. He asked how it happened and all I could think of was that it was my fault. I told Chuck that my friend couldn't stop his horse and it ran up on the concrete, and then I started crying so hard I couldn't talk. Chuck told me it was okay and that everything was going be all right. How the fuck could he know that? Why do people say shit like that? He didn't see, he didn't see. We rushed down the slope to where Bill was lying, and I was praying to God he wasn't dead and feeling it was all my fault. The feeling of guilt consumed me. When we reached Bill, there was a lot of blood, and Chuck said, "Oh my God," and I watched all the stupid optimism wash out of his face. He said we better not move him because we might make it worse. I didn't know how it could be any worse, and for a moment I felt like running away. I heard a siren in the distance and saw firemen, police, and an ambulance pull up in a cluster at the top of the hill. Then a fire truck and an ambulance pulled down the horse trail, just below where Bill lay in a heap. I felt dizzy, like I was gonna puke. I think I remember a stretcher and a couple of firemen lifting Bill onto it. I remember a policeman asking me what happened and Chuck standing there looking sad and saying, "What a shame." I thought yeah, shame on me, shame on me, it's all my fault. I saw he couldn't ride that well. I had told Sam to give him a good horse. Sadie! What happened to Sadie? Was she hurt bad, was she lying somewhere dying? I started yelling, "The horse, Sadie the horse." A policeman told me to calm down and that they had people looking for the horse. "Calm down, calm down," I repeated to myself, but I couldn't. I started crying again, thinking how pissed my mom was gonna be. Fuck, my life was shit. I was shit. Why wasn't it me and not Bill that was in the ambulance. I felt sorrier for myself than I did for Bill. I wanted to die. What if Bill died? What if Sadie died?

Two days later, the story was in the paper with both our names and a short bit on what happened. It was the first time I had seen my name in a paper, and it both excited and nauseated me. It said, "Bill was in serious but stable condition." What the fuck did that mean? I was too afraid to go to Bill's house because I knew his parents blamed me, and I couldn't face his brother, Bob. The article also said that Sadie had some contusions and a large laceration on her left hindquarter, but would be fine and back on the trail in no time. This made me feel a little better. At least I hadn't killed the horse.

A few more days passed, and I found myself in front of a desk in the hospital asking a nurse which room Bill Fox was in. I expected to get some kind of shit from her, like what was my relationship to the patient, but she didn't even look up. She just said, "Room 6F, down the hall on the right." As I walked down the hallway, looking in the rooms at all the sick people, all I could think was that F meant fucked. 3F fucked, 4F fucked, 5F fucked. I stopped in front of 6F. The door was open and I looked in. My knees buckled a little, and my heart was pounding as I stepped through the doorway and into the room. I couldn't tell if it was Bill. I looked back at the room number to be sure it was 6F. It was. Bill had bandages all over his head, except for his mouth and eyes. His leg was in a hoist thing with ropes and cables, elevated off the bed. His left arm was in a cast up to his shoulder. As I moved closer, I saw that his eyes were open and full of blood. I was told later by the nurse that's what happens sometimes when you have severe trauma to the head. He looked at me, but I'm not sure he recognized me, or anything else for that matter. He had a glazed look in his eyes, kind of like a newborn baby when you wonder what the fuck are they thinking or are they even thinking. I didn't know what to say, and I could feel the tears start to well up in my eyes. I thought it was better if I didn't have a breakdown in front of him; it would only make him feel worse. I turned around and walked out the door. 6F. F definitely meant fucked. I plodded down the hall and kept my head down, wiping the tears from my eyes. I glanced up for a minute and caught sight of Bill's parents walking toward me. Oh God no, why now? I wanted to throw myself on the floor and have a tantrum. I wasn't sure I could even control myself. I felt so ashamed and guilty. If there had been a window, I would have thrown myself out of it. I kept my head down and stared at the mint-green linoleum on the floor and thought it was a pretty color. The mind does weird shit when you're scared. It's probably why mint green is my least favorite color and even the sight of mint-green ice cream makes me cringe. I tried to make myself invisible, but my body felt like it weighed a thousand pounds, and I could hear my shoes clomp the floor with every step I took. We passed each other without a word. Maybe they were talking or not paying attention, or maybe I was invisible to them.

I never saw Bill's parents again, and when I would pass Bob at school, he would nod, but we never spoke. About a month after the accident, I saw Bill in the distance. He still had a cast on his arm. I avoided making eye contact with him; I felt too guilty to face him. Plus, I had heard he wasn't quite right since the accident, and I couldn't bear the thought of looking into those vacant, blood-filled eyes again. I never went back to the stable. I really missed riding and the smell of horse shit, but I knew Sam was mad at me, and I conjured up all kinds of scenarios of him yelling at me and telling me to get the hell off his property. I didn't ride a horse again for ten years. It was when I was an actor and got cast as a sharp-shooter in a Walt Disney TV special called *Kit Carson and the Mountain Men*. The best part of working on that show was I had my own horse for the three weeks we filmed, and I got to ride with some really great wrangler stunt men.

DEATH THREATS

Steve and I ran into Barry again and talked about that night and how we weren't into all the gay stuff. He said he understood, but he thought we were fun to hang out with and he liked driving us around. Steve and I didn't see any harm in that and liked cruising in the VW van. We both felt Barry was a decent guy. Barry would pick us up after school, and we would cruise through Bob's Big Boy and get an order of well-done fries with blue cheese dressing on the side. One afternoon, I saw Kathy Cremmo walking home from school with a friend. She was in my typing class, and I would catch her looking at me once in a while. I mentioned this to Barry and Steve. I guess I was bragging a little to make myself seem important or some shit. Barry told me to ask them if they wanted a ride, so I did. To my surprise, they got in. We hardly talked at all. Except we did set up a date for Saturday night with the two of them, and Barry agreed to drive us around.

We saw the girls waiting on the same corner where we had dropped them off a few days before. They looked different. They had makeup on, and both were wearing those pants that looked like they shrunk up in the dryer—"capris" is what they were called. Kathy had on a white button-up blouse that was tied at the waist and showed off her stomach. Barb was wearing a blue shirt that was tucked in. Kathy looked sexy but Barb looked kind of uptight. I got in the far back seat with Kathy, and Barb sat next to Steve. Kathy leaned up against me, but her friend Barb kept her distance from Steve. It seems like it's always like that, one girl is more friendly than the other with boys. Steve looked over his shoulder at me as if to say "what now?" I really had no idea what I was gonna do. Barry had bought us a couple of Country Club beers, so Steve and I cracked them open and shared them with the girls. It was awkward as hell, and none of us knew what to say or do, so we just drank the beers. Kathy was looking at me kind of weird, like, when are you gonna do something? I wasn't totally sure that was what she was thinking, but then she said in a whisper, "Stay up top and don't try to get in my pants." I said, "Sure." I had seen kids with hickies and thought that was the cool thing to do. So, I unbuttoned her blouse and started to suck her tits. She had huge boobs and I squeezed them as I sucked away. I gave her one on the left boob then finished off on the right boob. I fumbled with the bra hook but could never get it unhooked, so I just let it go. After years of practice, you get the hang of doing two things at once, unhooking and sucking, but not that night. I never even saw her nipples. The whole thing felt awkward and I have no idea what the fuck I accomplished. She didn't seem that excited about it and neither did I. We sat there listening to music as Barry cruised around. He really liked driving. Steve kept looking over his shoulder at me, and I could tell he was bored shitless and wanted to get rid of Barb. After about an hour, we dropped the girls off and we both jumped in the front seat next to Barry. Steve kept saying what a bummer she was and that she didn't want to do anything, not even make out. Barry tried to make Steve feel better and told him he could do a lot better than her. "What did you do?" Steve asked me. I told him I gave her a couple of hickies and that she had huge tits. I built it up to more than it was for some reason and felt bad for doing that. Then Steve asked if I saw her nipples. I told him it wasn't that big a deal and I didn't want to talk about it anymore. Barry threw his two cents in and said, "Girls are weird."

We did the drive-through at Bob's Big Boy and got some fries. Barry paid for them—he seemed to always have money. He told us his parents were wealthy and gave him an allowance. "Wow," I said, "You're twenty-six and still getting an allowance?" He told us he couldn't decide on a career and traveled the world with his parents. He said it was a good arrangement because they liked having him along because it helped divert their attention from each other, so they didn't argue as much. I guess in a way he was working. If I ever got an allowance for keeping my parents from arguing, I'd be a billionaire. Some people have it made. Because of all Barry did for us, we offered to wash the VW a couple of times, but he always said no. He really was a good guy.

Two days later when I met Steve on the corner, he was all worked up. He told me a badass Mexican guy came by his house asking about me and where I lived. Steve told him he didn't know and that he barely knew me except at school where sometimes we'd say hi. Steve's mother came to the door and asked the guy what he wanted and told him that he better not cause any trouble. She was a big, strong woman and wouldn't stand for anyone messing with her kids. The guy told Steve his name was Johnny Gonzales and he was gonna fuck me up because Kathy was his girlfriend. Steve's mom shut the door in his face and told him she would call the police if he came around again. Then she yelled at Steve for hanging out with me because I was a rabid Omitaa and I would infect him with my disease. I shouted, "What the fuck is a rabid Omitaa?" Steve told me it was a dog with rabies. The image hit home. Why did shit happen to me every time I got with a girl? Why did I get the girl that wanted me to suck her tits and not the one that kept her distance? I was beginning to think I was cursed. I took an oath that I wasn't gonna mess around with any girls for a while. I was scared shitless about what Steve had told me, and I asked around school about this guy. I figured if this Johnny Gonzales could find Steve's house, he could find mine. One guy told me he had heard about him and that he was a badass Vato gang member, from Toonerville, a place where a lot of Mexican gang members lived across the tracks. There was an urban myth that police wouldn't even go into that area because it was so deadly. I lived in fear of being stabbed to death by this guy for months.

We spent a lot of time at Frank's house and, one morning, when we walked up to the front door, it was ajar. It never was; it was always locked. We had gotten out of the habit of checking the garage for his parents' cars, but we took a quick look—both gone. We knocked and called his name. No answer. We called again. Still no answer. So we stepped inside and poked our heads into the kitchen. The TV was on as usual, but no Frank. We walked down the hall toward the bathroom thinking he might be taking a crap. It felt eerie, like something was wrong. Steve said, "What the fuck?" I said, "I don't know." Then Frank stepped into the hall. He was shirtless and wearing cutoff jeans, a black cowboy hat, and cowboy boots, with a holster buckled around his waist. He was pointing a gun at Steve's head. We froze. "Frank," I said softly. "Who the fuck are you?" he yelled. "What are you doing in my house?" I didn't know what Steve was doing; I was too afraid to look at anything except Frank and the gun. But I could feel Steve backing down the hall. Then all of a sudden, he bolted down the hall and out the front door. Frank let the gun drop to his side and started to laugh like crazy. What the fuck, what the fuck? "That's not funny. Are you crazy?" I said. He jerked the gun back up and pointed it at me. Then he dropped it to his side and started to laugh all over again. He held the gun to his head and pulled the trigger over and over as he said, "No bullets." I went down the hall and out the front door and saw Steve standing there ready to run if Frank came out with the gun. I told him he was just fucking around. He wasn't convinced till Frank came out and put the gun on the ground so Steve could hang onto it. Frank told us he trusted us and that the front door would be open from now on and for us to just come in. He made a fresh batch of donuts and let us eat them as they came out and not have to wait till the end. What a fucking weird way to let somebody know you trust them. I can tell you this, from that day forward, I never fully trusted Frank.

When I wasn't at Frank's, I would hurry home from school the back way, which meant climbing over a fence on the far side of the football field, just in case Johnny Gonzales was waiting for me in front of school. Weeks passed, and it's weird how things get buried in your brain, because one day after school this really tall girl, Linda Grise, asked me if I wanted to come over to her house and listen to records. I said, "Sure," like I didn't have some murdering son of a bitch out there stalking me wanting to cut my dick off. Linda sat next to me in social studies. She was very smart and had an accent. I never saw her walking around school with any girl-friends like most girls did. I wondered if it was because

she was so tall or because she was from another country. She had to be close to six feet. She was pretty, with
blondish hair, a pointy nose, and perfect lips. On the
walk home, I asked her where she was from, and she told
me she was born in Germany but moved here when she
was six. I asked her if she could speak German and she
spouted a few sentences. I laughed out loud at the sound
of it and she stopped abruptly. I think I hurt her feelings
and apologized a bunch of times and told her I loved the
sound of it. I really meant it, but I'm not sure she believed me. When we got to her house there was nobody
home. It was a nice apartment with doilies on the arms
of the sofa and chairs. I told her they were pretty, and
she told me that she and her mom crocheted them. She
sat cross-legged on the floor next to a pile of forty-fives
and picked one out and told me it was her favorite. She
turned on the record player, placed the forty-five on the
turntable, then set the needle gently on the record and
sat back to listen. She looked so cool sitting there. Her
skin was beautiful and she didn't have one pimple on
her face. I was amazed at how very delicately she moved
for such a tall girl. Most people who got so tall in high
school were klutzy, but not her. The song was "The Lion
Sleeps Tonight." At first I thought it was a girl singing

because the voice was so high, but Linda showed me the record cover, and sure enough, it was a guy. I loved everything about that song and couldn't get it out of my head for weeks. Even now when it comes on the oldies station, I have a rush of feelings. I still remember the words and sing along. We listened to a few more records, then Linda told me I better leave because her parents would be home soon. I stood at her door and said goodbye to her and apologized again for laughing. She smiled. She was very beautiful, and I enjoyed the time we spent together listening to music. I was never invited to her house again, but I will never forget her name, or our few blissful hours together listening to forty-fives.

TRACK

I have no idea why, but I decided to try out for track. I didn't have a clue as to what I would be good at. I missed starting day, but wandered onto the field after school one day. There were guys running sprints, others doing long jumps, and some guy off in the distance was pole-vaulting. I walked over to watch him. He counted his strides back from the bar, then turned and faced it. He found his grip on the pole, leaned forward, and stared at the bar. He looked very serious about all this, and I don't think he even noticed me standing there watching him. He took a few deep breaths, then took off like a bat out of hell, pole held high like a knight on a horse charging toward his opponent. When he got close to the bar, he dropped the front of the pole downward toward a box just below the bar and jammed it in. The pole bent, then whipped him upward. He seemed to just hang there in midair at the top over the bar. It was fucking amazing! He nicked the bar with his left arm just as he was coming down on the other side. The bar bent, sprung upward, then fell to the ground. He jumped up from the soft mats he had landed on and started cussing up a storm. I was so excited I thought I would piss myself. I wanted to try it so bad. I walked right over to him and said, "That was fucking amazing. Can I try?" He asked me if I had ever pole-vaulted before. I told him no, but that I had watched what he did and figured I could do it. He smirked at me and gave me a few tips on counting my strides to the bar. He showed me how to hold the pole properly and told me to kick my feet upward after I planted the pole. He also lowered the bar to eight feet. It had been set at ten. That made me mad because I had this idea in my head that I could make it over the ten-foot height. I measured out my strides, found a comfortable grip, stared at the bar, took a couple of deep breaths, and took off like a bat out of hell. It was harder than I imagined to run at full speed carrying that long pole, which was heavier than I would have thought. As I approached the bar, I let the front of the pole drop down and jammed it into the box. I kicked my feet upward and the pole bent—then sprung back straight. It sent me hurtling through the air, my arms and legs flailing wildly. Then all of a sudden, I stopped dead in midair, right over the bar. Oh fuck, I thought, and came crashing down on top of the bar. I landed half on the mats and half on the dirt. It knocked the wind out of me, and the poor kid watching thought I might have broken my back. But as soon as I caught my breath, I jumped to my feet and asked if I could try it again. Right about then the coach ran up and yelled, "What the hell do you think you're doing?" At first I didn't know who he was yelling at, but then I realized he was yelling at the both of us, but mostly at me. He ranted on about not just coming out here and trying stuff on my own, supervision, danger, shit like that. Then he told me I couldn't do it again. I told him I wanted to try out for pole vaulting and asked what I needed to do. He said nothing and that the season was under way and that I could run the 440, because that was the only opening he had on the team, but it was probably better if I waited till next year. I could tell he didn't like me and I didn't know why, but I knew better than to argue with him. So, I said, "Okay, coach." I don't know how I knew to say that, but it seemed to calm him down, and he walked away shaking his head.

A few days later, I was walking by a carpet store and noticed a bunch of bamboo poles stacked against the front of the store. Honest to God it was like a miracle.

I found out that they were used to roll carpets around to help stabilize them and make them easier to carry. I went in and asked the owner if I could have one. He asked what for and I told him to pole-vault with. He was not familiar with the sport, so I explained to him what it was. I guess I must have been pretty excited explaining it because he said okay, but if I got hurt not to come back and blame him. I got Steve to sneak me some tape from his house and wrapped the end of the pole where I held it. I ran back to the school with Steve, blabbing all the way saying, wait till you see this shit and maybe you could try it. He wasn't coordinated at all, and I knew he would suck at it, but I didn't tell him that because it would only make him feel bad. It was getting dark and there was nobody in sight on the field. We climbed over the fence and ran over to where the poles were, but the crossbar and the mats where gone. There were lots of trees lining the field, so I busted off a long, thin branch and used it as the crossbar. The mats were another problem, but I figured that I would try to land on my feet if I could. Steve shook his head and told me he thought it was dumb to do it without the mats. I knew he was right, but I wasn't gonna back down now. I had been bragging all the way to the school about how much of a natural I was and that maybe, if I practiced hard, I could convince the coach to let me be on the team and compete. I counted out my strides, turned and faced the bar, took two deep breaths, and charged at the bar. The pole felt lighter in my hands and I was able to run faster. I lowered the pole as I approached the bar and drove it into the box. I kicked my feet upward with a grunt. The pole bent, snapped in half, and I dropped backward—flat on my ass. Steve started laughing his ass off, but when he saw the look of disappointment on my face, he asked if I was hurt and told me I probably would have made it if the dumb pole hadn't snapped and that the poles they use must be a certain type of bamboo. He was probably right.

I entered the 440 race at school a couple of weeks later. I was a pretty fast runner and figured if I won maybe the coach would let me try pole vaulting. It was worth a try. I had never run in an organized race before, so I lined up next to four other guys and did what they did. I was nervous as hell because there were a lot of people in the bleachers watching, which I hadn't expected. I felt like puking, but just as I was having that feeling, I heard the crack of the starter pistol and off we went. Right out of the gates, a bulky dark-haired kid shot to the front. I stuck with him. I never did see the other guys after that.

It was pretty much me and the husky guy, who was surprisingly fast for his size. My legs started to burn, and I was sucking air, but I hung with him. We weren't running balls out, but pretty close. I started to feel weak, but I pulled up next to him on the inside as we rounded the corner and down the home stretch to the finish line. He was breathing hard and was about a stride ahead of me. Then he did it. He glanced over at me and I could see a look of fear in his eyes. I clenched my teeth and let out an animal growl as I flung myself past him and tumbled forward across the finish line—first place. I was rolling around gasping for air and damn near passed out. I pushed myself up to my feet and tried to walk it off, but I had to bend over and brace my hands on my knees to keep myself standing. I lifted my head and half expected to see people standing up and clapping for me, but nobody was standing and clapping. I did spot Steve in the bleachers jumping up and down like a fucking lunatic, and I felt proud. Then I saw the coach walking toward me. I stood up straight, put my shoulders back, and tried to control my breathing. I could feel my heart pounding with anticipation. I won the race. He was gonna give me a shot at pole vaulting. But he didn't congratulate me or offer me a spot on the team. He told me I was disqualified for passing on the inside and that what I did was dumb and dangerous. I said, "Fuck you," before he could get another word out and walked away. It was all I could do to hold the tears back. A few days later, a couple of football players cornered me in the restroom and tried to dunk my head in the toilet. They were tough fuckers, but I fought and screamed like a crazy motherfucker, and they finally gave up. Down deep I don't think they really wanted to do it. I saw the coach at the doorway and knew he had put them up to it. I don't know why that son of a bitch never liked me, but I know why I didn't like him. He was an asshole.

THE CANDY HEIST

It was late Sunday night, and Steve and I were heading home from Frank's house. We decided to hop the back fence at our school and cut across the field and through the school to get home. It knocked about ten minutes off the walk. It was dark as hell out, with no moon. It was a little eerie with no people around and so quiet we could hear the echo of our voices in the buildings. We made noises and listened as they floated back to us like the ghosts of students past. When we reached the wooden candy shack, we noticed the garage-like door was slightly ajar. We pushed on it and could see inside to where the boxes of candy were lined up on the shelves. We pushed harder, thinking we could break it off its hinges. The side door was padlocked, but there was no lock anywhere on the front hinged door. We kept looking around but didn't see anyone. It was dead quiet except for us pushing on the door. Steve took a running start at it and gave it a flying kick. It was loud as fuck and he fell back on his ass. It was comical but scary because I thought someone was gonna catch us for sure. We ran and hid behind an archway and listened. Nothing. We checked the door and one hinge was hanging by a screw. We had candy fever. Nothing was gonna stop us now. Steve took another run at it, flying at the wounded side with a right kick. The screw gave way and the door slumped inward. We ran and hid behind the archway and listened. Nothing. We made our way over to the shack and peered in. I squeezed through the opening and started handing boxes out to Steve. It was so dark I couldn't see what I was grabbing; I just kept throwing them out to him. Steve kept saying, "Enough, enough. How are we gonna carry all this shit?" I climbed out of the shack and looked at the giant pile of boxes and realized he was right. I pulled my shirt off and Steve understood and did the same.

We wrapped as many boxes as we could in our shirts. On the way home, I told Steve my mom saved all the bags from the market and that I would get a bunch and we could go back. But he said no way, he had plenty and he wasn't going to push his luck. We parted ways and I hurried along the dark and empty street to my house. I bounded up the stairs and knocked on the door. My mom always kept it locked. She took forever, but finally it opened slowly. I rushed in and dumped my stash on the kitchen table, grabbed a bunch of brown bags, and rushed back out the door. I heard my mom ask, "Where are you going?" I ran down the street back to the school and stood across the street for a few minutes to see if the police or anybody was around. There weren't even any cars, so l bolted across the street into the courtyard to the candy shack and started shoving boxes into the paper bags. I filled up six bags, but could only carry five, so I decided not to be greedy like the guy Dobbs in *The Treasure of the Sierra Madre*, who ends up getting killed in the end because he's so fucking greedy. I could barely walk carrying all those bags, but I made it home without a glitch and emptied the rest of the haul on the kitchen table. My brother woke up and came out and stood at the table drooling, but my mom told him he couldn't have one till the next day. I told her to let him have one, but she wouldn't relent, so he ran back to bed crying. She always managed to ruin even the good times. I went into our bedroom, got into bed next to him, and handed him a Snickers bar, telling him to unwrap it under the covers so Mom wouldn't hear. He asked me where I got them, but I told him to shut up and just eat it. He did, and I'll be damned if he didn't fall asleep before me. I had a hard time sleeping because I had eaten about three candy bars and must have been on a sugar high. I lay there for hours in that torturous state of mind, where no matter how hard you try, your brain just won't stop coming up with things to worry about. I thought about my uncle Al and how I never got to go to see the dogs race, and about my aunt Dottie's chicken and mashed potatoes, and that when I got old enough I would drive out there in my own car and visit them. Why couldn't they be my parents? I thought about my uncle Joe riding all over the country on the rails and wished I was with him. And I thought about my dad in jail. Then my mind went to the stack of candy on the table and how I could sell some around school for half price. Then Linda Grise drifted into my thoughts and "The Lion Sleeps Tonight" played in my head. The haunting melody soothed my mind. I imagined a lion sleeping in the shade under an ancient tree in the plains of Africa. Maybe someday I would go to Africa...with Linda.

DON'T CRY COYOTE

I woke up feeling afraid. I got dressed, grabbed a bunch of candy bars off the table, shoved them in my pockets, and left. I know my mom was awake, but she didn't say anything and neither did I. I felt like shit. It was barely light outside, dead quiet, and here I was walking around like a zombie. All I needed now was for a cop to come down the street and ask what I was doing. "Well, officer, I'm just out for my morning shit," I would say. "Stop being a smartass and answer the question or I'll throw your ass in jail," he would say. "Yes, sir," I would say and salute him. Then I thought, what if a cop did come and ask me to empty my pockets and found the stolen candy bars? I couldn't believe it. I went to bed with a head full of shit and woke up with it still there. I walked down to the corner where I usually met Steve and plopped my ass on the curb. I felt exhausted. My face felt droopy and I was hungry. I looked around to make sure there wasn't a cop, then pulled out a candy bar and took a bite. I started to cry. I was busy feeling sorry for myself when I saw something move out of the corner of my eye and looked up. At first I thought it was a mangy dog, but then I realized it was a coyote. He must have spotted me at the same time, because he stopped dead in his tracks, right in the middle of the street, and stared at me. I stared right back. He was a worn-out, nasty-looking fucker, and I felt like he was sizing me up, trying to figure out if he could eat me for breakfast. I felt a little afraid, but my adrenalin was pumping and I figured I could kill the fucker if he came at me. But he didn't. He just stared at me. I had seen coyotes at the Bronx Zoo before with my dad when I was a kid, but never out in the open. And then the strangest thing happened. He lowered his head, stretched his neck out toward me, stuck his nose up and out, and started sniffing. I realized he was smelling my damn candy bar. It made me laugh a little. The mangy son of a bitch was hungrier than I was. I unwrapped my candy bar and flung it in his direction. He didn't hesitate. He went right for it and gobbled it up in one bite. He stood there in the middle of the street staring at me. He had some sadass looking eyes and I felt sorry for him. I pulled another bar out of my pocket, unwrapped it, and flung it in his direction. Right in the middle of his gobbling that fucker up, the squeal of tires broke the silence as a truck came careening around the corner. I jumped to my feet and watched the truck run right over that poor bastard. "Nooo!" I yelled. But to my fucking surprise, it didn't touch one hair on his mangy-ass head. He bolted off behind a house and disappeared into the backyard. Now that's what you call a fucking miracle. I stood there laughing out loud, saying, "No way, no way." I sat back down and waited for him to come back, but he never did. I wanted to thank him for making me feel better. I could hardly wait for Steve to get there so I could tell him about the coyote. He was probably gonna tell me I was bullshitting, because shit like that just doesn't happen. My mind filled up with all kinds of thoughts about how that coyote could have been splattered all over the goddamn street and what would I have done? Would I have cleaned up his mashed body, or would I have just taken off and forgotten about the mess? Then I thought, what if that were me? Done, over, dead. I must have been sitting there thinking about this for a long time, because Steve came up behind me and slapped me in the head and said, "What's up, asshole?" He scared the crap out of me, and I yelled at him and told him he was an asshole. We talked to each other that way a lot; it was our way of saying we missed each other. On the way, as we hitched to Frank's house, I told him the coyote story, and sure enough, he told me I was bullshitting. First he said it would be impossible for a truck to run him over and not crush at least a leg or something. And besides, he had never seen a coyote in all the years he had lived in this neighborhood, which was since he was born. I swore to him it was the truth, but he said he wasn't going for it, because if he believed me I would just make fun of him for being such a sucker. He had a point. I did like to tease him about stuff, because he believed pretty much anything I told him. I couldn't help but think of the story about the boy who cried wolf all the time, but there was never a wolf, until one time there was, and nobody believed him, and I think he got his ass eaten. I laughed because the whole experience seemed funny and stupid. I was crying coyote and nobody believed me. But it's true. It really did happen.

THE BAY OF PIGS

When we got to Frank's house, he was in the kitchen. The smell of boiling oil and dough was in the air, and the TV was blaring in the living room. Frank was making his famous sugar donuts. He seemed a little more agitated than usual, so I tried to help by holding the bag open for him as he dropped more donuts in with a pair of metal tongs. I shook it up. It was filled with sugar, and the smell that came out of the bag made me almost lose control and just grab one. He dumped a few more in and said, "Okay." Steve and I dug in. They were hot so you couldn't just gulp them down or you would burn the shit out of your tongue. But fuck were they good. Frank didn't eat even one. He was too damn preoccupied with what was on the TV. He was goin' on about the Berlin Wall that was being built and how the commie bastards were closing in on us. Steve asked if the wall was in California. Frank told him to shut the fuck up. Then he started in about "Bahia de Cochinos"

(The Bay of Pigs). That's what he had been calling it for a while, Bahia de Cochinos. It did sound cool. And he went on about how Eisenhower and Kennedy where chickenshit for abandoning the men and that friends don't do that. I don't know what came over me but I yelled, "Bullshit!" I started ranting about how you never know when you're gonna die. That you could drop dead from a heart attack, or get cancer and rot away slow, or you could get smashed by a car. You never know, so you better live now and do whatever you want. So why don't we go free the prisoners from the fucking Bay of Pigs and quit talking about it? When I came out of my rant and looked at Frank, I saw a look of shock on his face. Steve looked dumbfounded. Frank said, "Okay." I looked at Steve. He said, "How do we get there?" Frank blurted out, "We'll take the Ford." Frank's parents had a '54 Ford that they had passed down to him, but his license had been revoked after his stay in the mental hospital and he couldn't drive, so it just sat parked on the side of the house. We sat around for the next couple of hours talking excitedly about the plan. Frank even poured us each a shot of Ten High, and we held our glasses up to toast Bahia de Cochinos, but Steve had a hard time pronouncing it right, so we finally just said fuck it and downed our shots and continued making our plan: scrounge together as much money as we could and leave late Friday night. Frank said his parents slept in late and probably wouldn't even notice the car was gone till they went to work on Monday. We all agreed that we would meet at Frank's house at 1:00 a.m. and made a pact not to tell anyone.

I spent the rest of the week moping around school and selling candy bars at half price. It was hard not to tell anyone about our plan to free the prisoners from the Bay of Pigs, because I felt pretty excited about it. Secrets suck. Whoever came up with the idea of secrets sucks. I've always hated secrets; they're different than lies. Lies you don't want anyone to find out about, but secrets you want to get up on a stage and yell, "I've got a secret and here it is!" And everybody would yell and clap and say what a great secret it was. I didn't tell anyone about our plan to free the prisoners from the Bay of Pigs until Friday. I was walking down the hall when Becca grabbed my arm and asked me to walk her to her class because Sharon was home with period cramps. She was always honest like that, and it made me want to tell her about my plan. What's the big deal I thought, it's not like she's gonna tell anyone if I ask her not to, and she probably wouldn't believe me anyway. I walked her to her class and she told me to have a nice weekend and she would see me Monday. Monday, hell, I'd probably be halfway to Cuba by then. I gave her a big hug which, by the look on her face, shocked her, and told her, "I would miss her." She didn't know what the hell I was talking about and said, "Sure." I felt like crap not telling her. See what I mean about secrets?

I made good money with candy bar sales that week, so that night I went to the market. I decided to splurge and stuffed some roast beef and provolone cheese down my pants and then bought a jar of dill pickles and a carton of chocolate milk for my little brother. We had a real feast that night, and my mom even laughed a little and didn't do anything to make the night any worse. I was happy about that because I already felt guilty that I was leaving my little brother behind, but I had no idea what I was getting into and didn't want to be responsible for him getting hurt. Thank God he fell asleep right away. I lay there for hours, then kissed him on the cheek and left.

When I got to the corner where Steve and I always met, he was already there. I asked if he was able to get any money and he told me he had four bucks. I had three fifty left from my candy bar sales. We hitched up to Frank's house and didn't talk hardly at all. I think we were both worried. We got to Frank's early, and I guess his parents had already fallen asleep because he came right out and it was only 12:30 by Steve's watch. Frank was wearing his black cowboy hat and a white T-shirt with a pack of cigs rolled up in his sleeve. He looked cool. He headed straight for the Ford. We pushed it out into the street so there wouldn't be any noise starting it up. Frank got behind the wheel, I sat in front, and Steve jumped in back. The Ford drifted down the hill, and when we got going fast enough, Frank popped the clutch. It jerked and the engine kicked in. I hollered, "Bahia de Cochinos," and Frank shouted back, "Bahia de Cochinos." Then Steve blurted out, "Bahia de Cochinos," and I'll be damned if he didn't get it right. We were on our way.

Frank smoked and drove for about four hours. Then he pulled over and asked me to take the wheel. I had only driven a stick once and didn't feel that good about it, but before I could respond Steve said, "I'll drive." Frank got out and Steve jumped into the driver's seat. I didn't know Steve could drive, but he was damn excited to get to it. The car was already on, but I guess he didn't realize that because he turned the key, and a scratching, whining sound made us all cringe. Frank yelled, "It's fucking on! You're gonna burn out the ignition." I didn't know shit about cars, but I knew that whatever Steve had done wasn't good. He grabbed the gear shift handle and attempted to put it in first, but it grinded like hell. Frank sat forward and yelled at Steve again. He asked him what the fuck he was doing and told him he had to put the clutch in. Steve wasn't saying shit. He just grabbed the gear shift again and tried to shove it into first. He didn't have the clutch in all the way, but he finally got it in gear and the Ford lurched forward—and stalled. Frank jumped out of the car and told Steve to get the fuck out of the car. I thought Frank was gonna kill him. To take the heat off Steve, I jumped behind the wheel and told Frank to take it easy and that I would drive. Frank finally calmed down and got back in the car. Steve got in the front seat next to me. He looked baffled and frightened. I don't know what the hell he was thinking. Did he think he could just jump behind the wheel and drive off into the sunset or some shit like that? I took a deep breath and let it out slow. Then I started the car. I pushed the clutch all the way to the floor, remembering what the Mexican guy had told me. I took hold of the gear shift and slipped it into first. I had been watching Frank all night and figured I could do it if I just went slow. Down for first, in and up for second, and straight down for third. I let the clutch out slow, and it revved a little too high when I released it. It jumped a bit, but we were moving, and at least I didn't stall it. Second gear was easier, but I did grind it a little. Third fell into place easily. Steve watched in awe as I drove down the highway. I could tell he was feeling like shit, so I asked him to turn on the music. Music always seems to make you feel better. "Hit the Road Jack" came on and I started belting out the words. I never could stay on key, but when the radio was blasting it didn't seem to make a difference. Frank was beating the back of the seat like a drum, and Steve started to slap out a beat on the dash. We were some rock 'n' roll muthafuckas. Why that song came on I don't know, but it was perfect. I thought about my uncle Joe and how when we got lucky and had a big haul of blue crabs he would always say, "Sometimes life throws you a bone."

I drove for a few hours and into Arizona. We were in a mountainous area, and I passed a sign that said: Flagstaff Ten Miles. I was too sleepy to keep driving, so I had to pull off the road. Steve and Frank were both asleep, so I rested my head back on the seat and conked out. I woke up shivering with a stiff neck. I had to blink a couple of times and focus my eyes, but sure enough, it was real. White flecks of snow were forming on the windshield. Frank sat up in the back seat and said, "I'm fucking freezing. Turn on the heater. Is that snow?" I said, "Yep," started the car up, and flicked on the heater. Steve woke up and yelped, "Snow!" He had never in all his life seen snow. Frank told me to get the car moving so the heater would get going—it was only blowing cold air. I went through the gears without a hitch; I was a natural. Snow started to build up on the windshield and quickly turned to ice. The windshield wiper started to slide over it, and soon I couldn't see out the window and had to pull over to scrape it off. But when I hit the brakes, we started to slide. And the whole time we were sliding, I was scared shitless because I felt I had no control. I just had to let the Ford do its thing. The damn beast finally came to a stop and all of us yelled, "Holy fuck!" at the same time, and then we laughed our asses off that we all said it at the same time. That's the thing about having a close call where you think you might die, but you don't. You're just so damn happy to be alive. It was cold as shit outside, but Steve volunteered to clear the windshield. He was happy as hell scraping snow and looking upward and opening his mouth to let the snow fall in. He was a funny fucker. Frank got behind the wheel; I didn't want any part of that icy shit. He would drive some, then pull over, and Steve would jump out and scrape away. After a while it wasn't fun anymore. We were all freezing our asses off, and the heater never did warm up. It was fucking miserable. I questioned myself and our stupid plan. We spotted a gas station, and Frank pulled in to see if they could fix it. He got out and talked to the mechanic. He must have told Frank he could fix it, because Frank jumped behind the wheel and pulled the Ford into the garage. The mechanic told us it would be about an hour. I guess Frank had enough money to pay for it, but it worried me. There was a coffee shop next to the gas station so we ran toward it. The ground was icy and Steve slipped and fell flat on his ass. It was funny as shit, and Frank and I laughed at the sight of it. Steve didn't think it was funny at first, but then he started to laugh too. We were all laughing and talking shit as we pushed our way through the door into the coffee shop. Oh beautiful heat. Thank God it was a warm, cozy, little place. We slid into an open booth, rubbing our hands together to get them to thaw out. Steve's fingers had a blue color to them, and I had a passing thought he might have frost bite, but I didn't say anything because I didn't want to freak him out. I remember seeing a movie once where a guy got frost bite and they had to cut his damn finger off. I really hoped Steve didn't have frost bite. We all ordered pancakes and coffee. When we got the coffee, we all held our hands on the mugs and let the hot coffee do its job. By the time the food got there, the color in Steve's fingers was back to normal. Frank told us how much it was gonna cost and not to worry because he had taken three hundred dollars from his stepdad's secret stash. Three hundred fucking dollars! We were rich. We ate pancakes, drank coffee, smoked, and talked about our plan. I had never drunk much coffee, and neither had Steve, so we got pretty wound up and jabbered on about how we needed more guns, a boat, shit like that. It's amazing how one minute you can feel like you're dying and the next you're flying high.

The snow had stopped by the time we walked back to the garage. The waitress told us it was a freak storm for this time of year and that as soon as we dropped down out of the high elevation it would warm up. Frank paid the mechanic, and when we got into the Ford, it was running and the heater was blasting. Frank drove. I didn't want any part of the sliding experience again.

He drove a few miles, and sure enough, when we got down to about two thousand feet, it warmed up and you couldn't even tell it had snowed. That was a relief. I thought of my dad and about how I would ride with him in the snow back East. I had a new respect for his driving skills and would tell him so when he got out. If I ever saw him again. I turned the radio on and "Onward, Christian Soldiers" was playing. I started singing, "Onward, Christian soldiers, marching off to war, with the cross of Jesus"— Frank flicked the knob. He didn't believe in God or any religion for that matter. He was an atheist. I liked "Onward, Christian Soldiers" and re-membered walking up the aisle in church carrying the cross. It was the only thing I really liked about being an altar boy, or church for that matter.

COMMIE BASTARDS AND TWO-HEADED GOATS

It was late afternoon when we crossed the border into New Mexico. Steve was asleep in the back seat. Frank was driving, smoking, and talking to me about Nikita Khrushchev, the commie bastard that ran Russia. He said Communism wasn't much different than our government in that everyone was supposed to be equal in Communism, and the government controlled all the money and would hand it out as they saw fit. In our government, a bunch of rich fuckers had all the money and controlled the government and told them how to dole it out. The difference was that in the US we could say fuck you and nothing would happen, but in Russia, if you said fuck you, your ass was thrown in jail and you were never heard from again. Either way, there's a bunch of crooked fuckers running the world.

My brain was straining to understand it all as I gazed out the window. Then I saw it, a giant billboard that said: Two-Headed Goat: The Incredible Zoo of Exotic and Bizarre Animals and Reptiles: Five Miles Ahead. "Two-headed goat!" I shouted. Steve sat bolt upright in the back seat and repeated my words. "Two-headed goat? Where?" Frank said it was a scam and he wasn't stopping, but over the next five miles the signs kept saying it over and over: Two-Headed Goat. Steve and I wouldn't let up. We begged, cussed up a storm, and called Frank a chickenshit if he didn't stop. As we got to the dirt driveway that led to the zoo, we thought Frank was gonna drive right by it, but at the last moment he swerved and slid into the parking lot, sending up a cloud of dust. He pulled to a stop, yanked the emergency brake on, and jumped out. Steve and I sat there for a moment, stunned. Then Frank hollered, "Come on, you fucking babies, let's go see the freak of nature." There was a six-foot wooden fence surrounding the zoo, with colorful pictures of all the creatures painted on it from top to bottom. Steve and I were so excited we were almost skipping. We got to the entrance and Frank handed the guy a buck fifty and we walked in. There were rattle snakes, a coyote that made me think of my coyote, a hawk, mice, and finally the cage with the two-headed goat. There was a crowd of people around it, and it took us a few minutes to get a good look. But when we got up close, we just stood there in awe. It looked like it had one head at first, but when you looked long enough, you could see the skull was heart shaped with four eyes, two mouths, two noses, and four ears, distributed equally on both sides. Frank said, "Fuck it," and walked away. Steve said, "Holy shit, that's kinda sad." My eyes filled up with tears. It was a freak, and I had that thought again: why does God do shit like this? I wiped my eyes. I didn't want anybody to see. People were laughing, and kids were giggling, and one guy was poking a stick at the poor little fucker. I went over and looked at a big lizard. "Fuck you, fuck you," I said to nobody in particular. As we walked back to the car, Steve was asking me if I thought it had two dicks, because the sign said it was a male. I told him to shut up. It made me think of my dick and that I was born with one ball. What if I were born with two dicks? Fuck, fuck, fuck.

When Steve and I got back to where the car had been parked, it was gone. We stood there looking around the dirt lot thinking we were in the wrong spot, but the lot was fairly empty, and this was definitely where we had parked. Then in the distance, we saw the Ford come racing across the dirt lot, straight at us, and I could see Frank's angry face through the windshield. He hit the brakes and slid up alongside us and growled, "Get in." He pulled out of the dirt lot, sending up a plume of dust, and skidded onto the highway, swerving wildly. I was hanging onto the door handle, trying not to be a chickenshit and scream, "Slow the fuck down." Frank said he was never gonna listen to us again about stopping and that somebody should burn that fucking zoo to the ground with all the animals in it. Things got dead quiet for a few minutes. Then Steve asked Frank if he thought the goat had two dicks? Frank started yelling, "Fuck you, you stupid son of a bitch," at the top of his lungs and looking in the back seat at him so his yelling could have the full impact. He almost drove us off the road and into a ditch, which he would have done if I hadn't grabbed the wheel and straightened us out. Frank was shaking more than I had ever seen him shake before. It scared me almost as much as the gun prank, and when I looked at the speedometer, we were doing ninety. I yelled, "Goddamn it, Frank, slow down." It took him a few seconds, but he finally calmed down and slowed the Ford to a decent speed. He asked me to light him a cigarette. I lit one and handed it to him. He took a long, deep drag and held it in for a long time, then blew it out slow. We never mentioned the goat again, even though it came into my mind and I knew Steve was thinking of it too. I just hoped he had enough sense to keep his mouth shut. I wondered what was in Frank's mind. I wondered if he felt like a freak of nature. I didn't want to burn the zoo down. I wanted to let all the animals go back into nature. I figured if the goat found other wild goats, they wouldn't have the same reaction as people, and they would accept him for what he was. But then I thought maybe they would kill him and that idea made me feel like shit. I don't know. I just know the only way I could stop thinking about that weird little fucker was imagining that he escaped somehow and found other wild goats that accepted him and he lived happily ever after. Then I remembered his head was shaped like a heart. Weird.

Texas went on forever. Frank had been driving and smoking for hours and hours. It had heated up a lot and we had the windows down. The hot, dry air blew our hair in all directions. It was boring as shit. There was nothing but static on the radio. And everything outside looked the same—dry brown rolling hills with oil wells sticking up all over. None of us were talking. I think we were all in a shitty mood. I was thirsty as hell, but didn't want to ask Frank to stop because he was in one of his moods. I knew he would have to stop for gas soon because the gauge was almost on empty. We passed a road sign that said: Houston Ten Miles. A couple of miles farther on, a sign said: Gas and Food: Two Miles Ahead. Thank God, because besides dying of thirst, I had to piss like a race horse, a term I picked up at the stables. Buck used it a lot. He said it was because when a horse pissed it looked like a fire hose gushing water out. He was right; it was always a sight to see, especially on the males. Their dicks did kinda look like a fire hose, and when they would start gushing, you didn't want to be anywhere near because when that stream of water hit the dirt it would splash crap up all over you.

Frank pulled into the gas station and up to the pump. I jumped out and ran inside to take a piss. Steve got out and started pumping gas. That was his job unless he was sleeping. Maybe he liked doing it because Frank would never let him drive and it made him feel like he was doing his part. Steve wasn't lazy; he was just a little slow. I got out of the bathroom and saw Frank at the counter buying a bunch of stuff. Steve was trying on big black cowboy hats. I walked over to him and he stuck one on my head. They had a little mirror you could look in. I thought I looked stupid, but Steve said I looked like a wrangler. He was wearing one himself and it looked natural on him. I put the hat back and walked up to the counter to see what Frank was getting. He had a bunch of ice cream sandwiches piled up, some chips, beef jerky, and a gallon of water. Frank had a good heart. He didn't have to buy the jerky; he hated the whole idea of meat. The girl behind the counter was slow bagging up our stuff, and I looked around for Steve but didn't see him anywhere in the store. Weird. We walked out to the car and saw Steve sitting in the back seat with a big shit-eatin' grin on his face. I got behind the wheel and pulled out of the parking lot. I caught a glimpse of Steve in the back seat. He was wearing that big black cowboy hat and smiling ear to ear. He reached down and pulled another one off the floor and stuck it on my head. Now all three of us had black cowboy hats. Frank smiled and we all dug into those ice cream sandwiches. I turned on the radio and "Quarter to Three" was playing. We all started snapping our fingers and singing. None of us knew the words, so we were all singing different shit, but it didn't seem to matter because we were having fun.

SELF-DOUBT, ALLIGATORS, AND HOPE

As the sun went down, I drove past a sign that read: Louisiana State Line. Frank and Steve were both knocked out, and I could feel my head drop every so often, then jerk me awake. I don't know how long I fucked with our lives in that half-asleep, half-awake state of mind, but my head snapped back so violently once, when I was half off the road, that I had to jerk the steering wheel to keep from crashing into a ditch. I forced my eyes open and found a spot to pull off. I stopped under a giant weeping willow tree, adrenaline pumping. I took a few deep breaths and realized I hadn't seen a car for miles and wondered if I had dozed off and taken a wrong turn somewhere. Frank sat up, yawned, and asked if there was something wrong. I told him I was fuckin' tired and couldn't drive anymore and that maybe I took a wrong turn somewhere. Steve sat forward and said, "Hungry." So we made some bologna and cheese sandwiches.

Frank just ate the cheese of course. We topped it off with a whole jar of dill pickles and washed it all down with a quart of Coke. Steve had walked out of the last market with four big bottles. Frank got out and walked to the back of the car and opened the trunk. He came back with a bottle of Ten High Whiskey. He opened it and took a big gulp and followed up with a swallow of Coke. Steve went big, but gagged it up and spit it all over the car. The surprising thing was Frank didn't yell at him. He just said quietly, "Let's sit outside." So we got out and sat on some logs. There was a giant full moon and the sky was full of stars. Fireflies flicked off and on, and we oohed and aahed, trying see who could point to one as soon as it flicked on. It was so dark, we could barely see one another's faces, but it made things, the world, our world, seem small in a way, and I liked that. Steve apologized for spitting up all over the car and handed me the bottle, and I took a slug. It was nasty shit and it took two giant slugs of Coke to get that wretched taste out of my mouth. Steve tried again and held it down this time, barely. I came up with the idea that when we drank we had to smile and act like it tasted great. Frank took the bottle and took a good-sized gulp and smiled a pain-ful looking smile, like somebody had kicked him in the balls. I went next. I held the bottle up, inspected the label, and said, "Damn fine whiskey. Cheers, boys." I took a slug and said, "Ah," a big smile on my face. Both Frank and Steve laughed their asses off, and we spent the next hour fucking around trying to outdo each other. Steve was no good at this game. As hard as he would try, after every swig he would get a gag-puke look on his face, and I swear once he puked in his own mouth, swallowed it, and smiled. Frank and I were dying laughing. I had never seen Frank so happy and it made me feel good. Frank won when he took a swallow, stood up, and yelled, "Heil Hitler," in a German accent. He was drunk as shit, and when he threw his arm up in that stupid Nazi salute, he fell backwards over the log, slammed on his back, and knocked the wind out of himself. It was a scary moment. If you have ever had the wind knocked out of you and couldn't breathe, you know what I'm talking about. It feels like you will never breathe again. When he finally got his breath back, we set him back on his log and told him he won.

Then the mood changed. Things got serious in the way they can when people get drunk. Steve asked how many prisoners there were. Frank slurred, "Two thousand or something." I jumped in and said, "You told me twelve hundred." Frank said, "Sure." Steve said, "We're gonna need a huge boat." Frank said, "An ocean liner." I didn't like where the conversation was going, and I was starting to feel bad. Frank said, "We're not gonna be able to do much with just one gun." "How far is Cuba from Florida?" Steve asked. "Only a hundred miles from Key West," I said in a real positive way. But the mood didn't change. Frank was looking out into the darkness, and Steve asked what he was looking at. Before he could answer, I jumped in and said, "Maybe we can't get them all out, maybe just a couple of hundred. We could hijack a fishing boat with a captain, and we could steal more guns somewhere." I could tell they were drunk, and they both had that fucking feel sorry for myself look on their faces that drunks get when they feel lonely as shit and hopeless. As if things weren't bad enough, the moon slipped behind a cloud as if to say fuck you, idiots. We could barely make out one another's silhouettes. It was so quiet we could hear the mosquitoes buzzing around our heads. The darkness would blink with an occasional firefly, but even that didn't make any of us feel any better. Then we heard a rush of grass. Steve yelled, "Alligator," and jumped onto the hood of the car. I was right behind him, then Frank. We were all drunk and scared, so we were clawing over each other like a bunch of spazzes trying not to get eaten. We all searched the area surrounding the car to see if we could see him, but we couldn't see shit because the clouds were still blocking the moon. Frank asked Steve if he was sure he saw an alligator, maybe it was a possum or something. Steve didn't say anything for a minute. Then he said, "I'm pretty sure." So we sat there for a while and waited. The moon finally came out from behind the clouds and we could see pretty good. No sign of an alligator. Frank had started to slide down off the car when a big ass alligator lifted its head out of the grass and looked up at him. Frank pulled himself back up and we all clambered to the roof. I had never seen an alligator, in the zoo or out, but I can tell you they are some scary dinosaur-looking fuckers, especially when you're stuck on the roof of a car, in the dark, in the middle of nowhere, and those ugly bastards are sitting there drooling, waiting for you to come down so they can eat your ass. The son of a bitch put his head back down and waited. His eyes closed, and he didn't move a muscle for at least an hour. We thought he might be asleep. No way did I want to stay on the roof of the car all night, so I slid down onto the hood and watched that ugly bastard's closed eyes. Just as I was about to step on the ground, his eyes rolled open. It's like he had food radar or some shit. I crawled back up on the roof and settled in. We talked about how fast alligators could move, and Steve said he heard somewhere that an alligator ran down a dog once for almost a block and finally caught the poor sucker and swallowed it whole. It sounded like bullshit, but neither Frank nor I were gonna chance it. We were all sloppy drunk and dead tired, so we took turns sleeping. One of us was always awake in case anybody started to slide off. That way we could catch him. I woke up at first light, and I'll be damned if Frank and Steve weren't both asleep. I knew Steve had the last watch, so I nudged him, because if Frank found out he had fallen asleep, he would probably have a shit fit. Steve asked me in a baby voice, "Is the gator gone?" I snapped at him, "I don't know. You were supposed to be watching. And I don't know why, but it irritates me that you call it a gator, dumbass." He had a guilty look on his face, so I told him not to worry, I wouldn't mention it to Frank. He dropped his head and I felt bad for busting his balls, but damn it, one of us could have been eaten. We nudged Frank because I couldn't stand being on the roof for another minute, plus, I had an idea. Frank woke up and I explained my idea to him, and he thought it was good. I pulled off one of my shoes and tossed it on the ground where we had seen the alligator last. Nothing: no head, no demon eyes. I slid down to the hood and looked around for a minute. Frank nodded and said, "Looks okay." Steve did the same. I wasn't going for my shoe; I was going for the inside of the car. My plan was to get down, grab the door handle, pull it open, jump inside, and shut it quick behind me. I wasn't gonna go slow and quiet; I was gonna be the "Flash." I hit the ground, put my hand on the door handle, and yanked it open. Frank yelled, "Alligator." I banged my head getting in and slammed the door behind me. I looked out the window expecting to see that ugly bastard at the door, but no alligator. Frank was just fucking with me. He really had a sick sense of humor, and I made an oath to myself to get him back. Frank jumped down on the driver's side, and Steve got in the back. He had grabbed my shoe for me because he felt bad about what Frank did to me, and for falling asleep I guess. It was a good gesture.

Nobody talked for a long time. I was brooding, thinking how I could fuck Frank up. I didn't care if he lost his mind; I was tired of his bullshit pranks. He was just mean sometimes. I turned on the radio, but some sad shit was playing, so I shut it right off. My brain was pounding, my neck was stiff, I felt miserable. But when I glanced over at Frank, he looked even more miserable than me, and that made me feel good. Steve had fallen asleep in the back seat. All in all, it was shit.

Frank had been driving for hours and we hadn't spoken a word. Then Steve sat up in the back seat and said, "Hungry." It wasn't cute or funny at all. Fuck you, I thought to myself, all you do is eat and sleep. What good are you? Then Steve shouted, "Dairy Queen!" I didn't think Frank was gonna stop, but he surprised me. We all jumped out and went up to the window. Frank got a grilled cheese with fries and a root beer float. Steve got a cheeseburger with fries and a chocolate shake. I did the same. We sat at a wooden picnic table and just looked at each other. It was a sickening feeling. Frank said, "Maybe we should go back." "I'm not going back," I shot at him in an angry voice. Steve just sat there looking confused and scared. It was a long, tense, quiet moment. The girl at the window called out, "Number seven!" Steve boomed, "Seven's a lucky number!" He jumped up and walked to the window. He was talking so loud we could hear him when he told the girl at the window, "That's us, seven is our lucky number!" Frank and I just looked at each other and shook our heads. I think we both wanted to smile but didn't. Steve set the food down, looked at both of us, and said, "Why don't you two assholes just shut the fuck up and eat?" What he said made no sense, and was so awkward and ridiculous, that Frank and I couldn't keep from cracking up. We ate our food in silence, sucked down our drinks, then got back in the Ford. Frank pulled out of the driveway, turned left toward Florida, and said, in a melodic whisper, "Bahia de Cochinos." I almost broke down, but I managed to squeak out, "Bahia de Cochinos." Steve yelled, "Bahia de Cochise." I don't know if he was fucking around or just so excited he mixed up the word, but we all started laughing and making Indian hoots and howls. We screamed, "Free the Indians! Death to the white man!" And other shit like that. We were back.

I was at the wheel, Frank was knocked out in the back seat, and Steve was trying to get some tunes on the radio. The highway was lined on our right with palm trees that arched inward from the ocean. A warm, salty breeze filled the car with a dreamy calm. The ocean was a shimmering blue-green and the sand a glistening white. It looked like a mirage or one of those postcards that makes a place look so perfect you just want to be there. I thought fuck it and pulled over. I yanked on the parking brake and shut the Ford off. I turned to see if Frank was awake. He was in such a deep sleep that drool dripped out of the corner of his mouth. I was glad to see he was sleeping, but it was a little disgusting. There was nobody in sight on the beach or in the water. It was deserted. I pulled off my shoes, socks, and shirt; Steve did the same. We climbed out the open windows so we wouldn't wake Frank by opening and shutting the doors and ran balls out through the hot sand. Steve was yelling, "Go, go, go." I was giving it right back, "Go, go, go." As we got close to the water, we pulled off our pants, tripping and laughing like hell, never losing our forward momentum toward the blue-green water that was drawing us in. We hit the water at the same time, but Steve tripped over himself and fell face first. I laughed out loud and threw myself headlong into the water. There is nothing like the feeling of jumping butt naked into the ocean; it just makes you happy to be alive. I swam out a way, flipped over on my back, and floated there, looking up at the sky. It was so quiet with my head half under the water, and I felt such peace that I wondered if this was what it was like in the womb. Why I had that thought I don't know. I had never thought of my mother as being peaceful, only agitated and mean. But maybe there was a moment when she was happy I was in her belly. I floated and let my mind drift, no thoughts, only the sound of water in and out of my ears and the blue sky above—then two hands clamped on to me. One on my face, the other groping my chest, trying to take hold. I heard Steve gasping, "Help, help," just before he shoved my head under water. I fought free of his death grip and came up gasping for air. He came at me again, gulping water, gagging, yelling, "Help me." I yelled, "Calm down, calm down. I got ya." I held him up and told him to look at me. I repeated, "I got ya," in a calm voice. His eyes were jumping all over the place. "Calm down," I said again in a slow whisper. "Breathe in, breathe out, in, out, in…" Little by little his eyes slowed and his body relaxed. He got that goony smile on his face that I loved, the smile that made him my best friend. I told him to kick his feet and relax. Everything was fine after that, and he told me he didn't know what had happened. We just kicked around in place for a while, and I told him about some guy who was drowning in a lake and a lifeguard pulled him out. I asked the lifeguard what happened and he explained to me that people hyperventilate, which is a fancy way of saying they breathe in, but they don't breathe out. So they just keep on breathing in till they start to sink, which is what happens when you take in too much air. He liked the story and it seemed to calm him down even more. I tried to teach him how to float, but it was useless. Maybe some people just can't; maybe some people just sink.

We spotted Frank standing on the beach in a pair of cut-off jeans. I was worried he would be pissed, but he waded in, dunked his head under water, and when he came up he let out a howl. Steve and I swam to where Frank was splashing around. I hung with Frank while Steve stumbled out of the water and dropped down in the hot sand. I think his near drowning wore him out. I splashed around with Frank for a long time. Then we walked out and plopped down in the hot sand next to Steve, who had fallen asleep face down in the sand. I pulled the sand in around my chest and looked out at the ocean.

It reminded me of when I was little and would go to Far Rockaway Beach with my dad and little brother. My brother and I would run in and out of the water in our underwear for hours while my dad would sit in the sand with his shirt off. His face and arms were dark brown, but his body was scary white where his shirt covered it at work. He was a painter by trade and spent a lot of time in the sun. His pants were rolled up to his knees and he looked kinda funny sitting there. But we weren't the worst lookers on that beach. It was always packed with people of all sizes and shapes, wearing all kinds of outfits. Some in swim suits, some in underwear like my little brother and me, and some just went in the water with all their damn clothes on. There were even some kids our age running around butt naked, and once I even saw a woman in nothing but her bra and underwear. She had huge boobs and was jumping up and down in the water and one of them plopped right out. She stuck it back in quick, but was laughing so hard the damn thing plopped out again. She saw me looking at her and laughing and smiled at me and kept right on laughing. That was the thing I loved about Far Rockaway, everybody was having such a damn good time. I guess that's the magic of the ocean, people let it all hang out. Then out of nowhere, my dad would jump to his feet and race to the water's edge and do a flying flip into the water, swim out under water for an unbelievable distance, pop his head up, and flip his black hair out of his face. I laughed at the sight of it every time he did it. I was so proud of him. Dad was an athlete. He was really quick, lean, and muscular. Wherever there was a pull-up bar in a park or at the beach, he would leap to it and do all kinds of tricks. He could even do a giant, which is where you swing straight up and into a handstand on the bar. Then he would swing around a couple of times, release, fly through the air, and land on his feet. I don't know how he did it or where he learned to do it, but it was amazing to watch.

We all must have dozed off in the hot sun, because I woke up to the sound of voices. An old suntanned leather-faced guy with a scraggly white beard and short, buzzed hair, wearing nothing but a pair of worn-out, baggy tan shorts, held up by a thin piece of rope that hung well below his belly, stood over me like an over-sized dwarf. Hanging on his arm was a pretty woman half his age. She had short blonde hair combed back and golden suntanned skin, mostly exposed because of the skimpy bathing suit she wore. The woman said, "Doin' a little skinny dippin'? Be careful not to burn your tush, it's looking a bit red." I said, "Sure," but I sure as hell wasn't gonna get up and put my pants on with them standing there watching. The old dwarf spoke in a gravelly, deep voice, "Oh, to be young and back in Saint Tropez." The woman said, in a wistful voice, "You'll always be young, lover boy," as she tugged gently on his arm and led him down the beach. Steve was awake now, and Frank said,

"Let's go. I'm hungry." I was covered in sand, so I walked down to the water and watched the couple in the distance, walking arm in arm, and wondered if that was what they did every day. I rinsed off and Steve did the same. Then we started screwing around—splashing, wrestling, and trying to dunk each other, till we heard Frank yell, "I'm leaving." Trying to get my pants on without getting sand in the legs was not easy. Steve got one leg in his and then fell back on his ass and had to go back in and rinse off. Frank told him to quit fuckin' around, but I don't think he was. He just wasn't that co-ordinated. We were both laughing and Frank got fed up and said, "Fuck it, I'm goin' without you two idiots." He got grumpy when he was hungry.

We hadn't gone far when Frank pulled off the road into a dirt lot and stopped in front of an old wooden shack. It was a colorful looking shanty, with weath-ered orange and blue paint worn through to the wood in spots. A bright yellow sign hung over the entrance. Scrawled across it in black letters was written: Rosie's. Just under the name it said: Best Shrimp & Grits on the Coast. Off to the side of the shack, green, yellow, and orange cloth panels floated in the gentle breeze above a couple of long wooden benches. A group of people was just leaving as we walked through the squeaky screen door into the tiny shack. We were greeted by a large black woman who said, in a slow Cajun drawl, "Afternoon, gentlemen. I'm Rosie." Her voice was like velvet, and the deep, sweet, melodic tone reminded me of Nat King Cole and Christmas songs, which was weird because it was hot as hell and muggy. She wore a long, colorful caftan and had a giant head of wild, curly black hair with a pink scarf knotted on her forehead that made it stand up and back off her face. Large gold hoop earrings hung down to her shoulders, and she had a small red stone stuck in the side of her nose. She said, "Inside or out?" "Is there a menu?" Steve asked. "Shrimp and grits like the sign says. You can get it twenty different ways, but it's still shrimp and grits. And if you good customers, I get you some of my homemade beignets." Frank said, "Fine, we'll sit outside." That surprised me, because I didn't have any idea what grits or beignets were, but I thought for sure shrimp was in the meat category. We sat outside and Rosie brought us out a pitcher of lemonade and three glasses. While she poured us each a big glass, she spoke in a singsong voice and gave us the list of different sauces you could get on your shrimp and grits. Frank picked curry, Steve pineapple. When Rosie spoke, her eyes sparkled with joyful peace, and her honey voice was so pleasant that I was completely hypnotized by her. When my turn came, I had no idea what she had said. I just sat there slack-jawed, looking up at her. She smiled the most loving smile anyone's ever smiled at me and said, "What's it gonna be, good lookin'?" I don't know where my mind had gone, or how long it was before I finally said, "What?" Frank barked, "Pick one. I'm starving." Rosie was looking deep into my eyes, and for a minute I thought I was gonna cry. Then she said, "Rosie's gonna get you her favorite." All I could say was, "Sure," and I watched her drift off back through the squeaky screen door humming to herself. I wondered if she was an angel. The cloth panels flapped softly… the salty smell of the ocean…the swaying palm trees; I felt like I was in heaven. Frank was explaining to Steve what grits were but said he had no idea about the beignet thing. I lay down on the bench and stared up at the cloth panels. The sky was a soft blue, with puffs of cotton clouds. One cloud looked like an old pirate ship with billowing sails. I thought of Rosie and her peaceful eyes and how she made me feel...

I could have lain there forever, but the squeaky screen door alerted me to Rosie's return. She placed our grits and shrimp on the table, along with a spoon and a cloth napkin for each of us. I sat up just as she set my bowl in front of me. She watched me as I picked up my spoon and took a bite. I had never tasted anything like it. The shrimp and sauce were spicy-sweet, and the grits seemed to calm everything down, and I'll be damned if it didn't move into first place over my aunt Dottie's chicken and mashed potatoes. Sorry, Aunt Dottie. Rosie said, "I told you so, good lookin'," and hummed her way back into the shack. We all sat there eating, making moaning sounds. I asked Frank why he was eating shrimp. He said, "It's okay to eat shrimp." I knew better than to question him, because he always got pissed off when you asked about his eating. I thought it was bullshit and that he was hungry and didn't care what he shoved in his mouth. I was still mad at him about the alligator, and this made me feel I had something on him. None of us left anything in our bowls, which made Rosie happy. She said, "That's the best compliment I can get from a customer, next to a big tip," and laughed. She came back out with a plate stacked with white powdered donuts. She told us they weren't donuts, but "beignets."

Frank was particularly interested in them because he considered himself to be quite the donut maker. They were hot, light as air, and hollow in the middle, and every time you took a bite, a little puff of powdered sugar would float out from it. Frank was impressed. When Rosie came back out, he told her he was pretty good at making beignets himself, but hers were far superior. She told him that was a very generous and kind thing to say. Frank blushed a little, then paid the bill and told Rosie to keep the change. He remembered what she'd said about the big tip. We all thanked her a bunch, and as we walked to the car, I felt a brush of cool air on my neck, as if someone was blowing on it, and it made me shudder. I stopped for a moment, then turned and walked back inside the shack. Rosie was standing at the small counter folding napkins. Once I was face to face with her, I felt stupid. I wasn't sure why I had come back in. She looked at me for a long time, then came over and put her arms around me. Tears rolled down my cheeks, and as hard as I tried, I couldn't get them to stop. Rosie didn't let go; she just held me till I stopped my whimpering. Then she took my face in her soft hands and said, "Lache pas la patate." She told me to repeat it. I said, "Lache pas la patate." She smiled and said, "Good, good."

She told me it was a Creole saying and it meant don't drop the potato, which meant don't give up. She kissed me on the forehead and said it again, "Lache pas la patate. Now you say it." I repeated it. "Lache pa la patate." Then I turned and walked out the squeaky screen door. As I walked back to the car, I said it out loud. "Lache pas la patate. Lache pas la patate." I'll be damned if I wasn't speaking Creole. I hopped in the back seat and Frank pulled out on the highway. Steve asked why I went back inside, and I told him I was trying to get her to tell me how she made the beignets, but that she wouldn't give up her secret. I rolled down my window and looked out at the palm trees and the weeping willows. Lache pas la palate, don't drop the potato, don't give up. The palm trees reminded me of Rosie, bending gracefully in the breeze, with their fronds at the top. I looked at the beautiful weeping willow trees and thought their roots went deep into the earth and that the full, slumping branches were life. That's what Rosie was: everything good about life. I could feel my eyes well up and had to grit my teeth to make the feeling stop. I didn't want Frank or Steve to see what a baby I was. I had heard about Creole voodoo magic in the South and felt like Rosie had cast a spell on me. In all my life, in all the different churches I had attended, and even when I was an altar boy, I had never felt so much love. So, I thought if it was voodoo magic, the whole world should be under its spell.

THE STORM

We crossed into Florida and all hell broke loose. Dark clouds came out of nowhere and it started to pour. Lightning lit up the skies all around us, and every crack of thunder seemed to explode right on the roof of the car. Frank was driving about twenty miles an hour because he could only see about ten feet in front of him. We inched along like this for hours, all of us sitting up in our seats, waiting for the next boom of thunder. In all my life, I had never experienced anything like it; it was scary and exciting at the same time. When the lightning struck, the sky seemed to vibrate as the bolt lit it up. Then the boom of thunder would hit, and Steve and I would scream every time. I don't think Frank thought it was exciting, because he was too focused on driving. But damn was it fun. The idea of getting electrocuted to death every few minutes and then not dying was exhilarating. The lightning was death, the boom life—that's why we screamed when it boomed; it meant we were alive. This went on forever, till Frank pulled into a town called Saint Petersburg. He pulled up in front of an outdoor cafe that had a metal hooded roof covering the tables. We jumped out of the car and bolted inside, but we still got totally soaked. It was no Rosie's, but the prices were dirt cheap. We sat at an open table, and I noticed almost everyone, yeah everyone but us, was old. I mean like seventy or eighty years old. Even the waitress was ancient. I honestly don't know how she carried the plates. A couple of times she did trip, and I jumped up to keep her from falling. She was a grumpy, old witch and told me she was fine and didn't need my help. Okay I thought, drop all your shit and break your ass, see if I care. The rain pounded down on the tin roof, but nobody seemed to pay attention. Or maybe they were deaf, or maybe old people don't give a shit about stuff like that, but I can tell you it irritated the hell out of me. Frank ordered some vegetables, and boy did the waitress make a big deal out of that. She asked him like three times what he wanted as a meat: beef, chicken, or pork? He started to simmer, and to keep things from going bad I said, "How are the burgers?" She said, "Is that a trick question?" Rather than get into it with her I said, "I'll take a burger with everything." She snapped back,

"It comes with lettuce, tomato, and onions on the side."
Steve said, "I'll take the same, and can I get some pickles?" She never responded; she just turned and hobbled
away. I looked around and watched several of the old
people eating watermelon. The thing was, they ate it
rind and all. I had never seen anything like it. I had been
told it was not good to eat the rind because it would give
you diarrhea. If that was true, this whole city was gonna
be hit by not only a rainstorm but a shitstorm. I laughed
to myself at the thought of it. I thought of a story Buck
had told me about a rainstorm he had experienced in
Texas. He said it was a "horse piss storm" because when
a horse pisses it's like a fire hose blowin' water out, not
just drops comin' down. He told me it was like a thousand horses letting loose from heaven. He always used
horses as a way to describe things. I missed the stables,
and Sam, and Buck, and Cloud. Then I thought of my
friend Bill, and that put me in a real shitty mood.

The burgers came out along with Frank's veggies.
Of course she forgot Steve's pickles, and when he asked
for them again she said there would be an extra charge.
Steve said, "Forget it," and she shuffled off. We ate the
shit food; it was the worst yet on our trip. We all got
a big slice of watermelon though, and I guess that was

their specialty, because it was nice and cold and sweet as could be. I ate pretty far into the white part, but no way was I gonna eat the rind. The rain kept pounding the tin roof, and I couldn't wait to pay the bill and get the hell out of there. While we were waiting, some old guy from the table next to us leaned over and asked if he could have the rind. We slopped it all on one plate and Frank handed it to him. The old guy said, "Best part." I thought, happy shitstorm. The old grump dropped off the bill. Frank paid it and didn't leave a tip. As much as I didn't like her, I felt bad about the no tip thing. A friend of mine's sister was a waitress, and she told me that's how she made her money—off tips. If I was a waiter, I would kiss everybody's ass so I could get a good tip. What that old grump was doing was just dumb. We stood at the edge of where the tin roof ended, waiting to see if the horse rain was gonna stop: no luck. I was gonna drive, Steve was shotgun, and Frank was in the back. We all flew to the car, yanked open the doors, and threw ourselves inside, soaked.

I had been driving for a couple of hours at about twenty miles an hour, and it was really miserable sitting in our wet clothes with all the windows closed. The Ford didn't have air, and it was raining so damn hard that when you rolled down the window, it was like somebody tossed a bucket of water in at you. Frank told me to pull into the Rest Easy Motel with the flashing red vacancy sign. He ran into the office and came out with a room key. We pulled up in front of number seven. Steve started right in with the lucky number seven shit, but Frank and I were wet, tired, and in no mood for his blabber. Frank opened the door and there were two beds with a night stand and a light in between, and a couple of hooks to hang stuff on. The room had a musky smell, but it was good to get out of my wet clothes. Frank got in the shower first. I got in next and let the hot water run on my head and neck for what must have been a long time, because Steve yelled for me to leave him some hot water. Frank claimed one bed for himself, so when Steve came out he hopped in bed next to me. He yanked the sheet off me onto himself. I shoved him off the bed and he banged on the floor. He jumped back in the bed, and we fought and pushed and used our feet to try to shove each other off the bed. We were laughing like a couple of idiots when Frank finally got tired of our bullshit and told us to knock it off. It took a couple of more shoves and Frank moaning, "Please stop," before we settled down. I could tell Frank was tired, so I let Steve have the last push and that was all it took. He was asleep in minutes. I could hear Frank in the next bed, and his even breathing told me he was out too. I lay there for a long time. I couldn't get my mind to slow down. Every time I thought I was gonna doze off, some new idea would come into my head. I knew we were gonna be in Key West tomorrow sometime, but I didn't want to think about all the details with the guns and the boat and all, so I decided to just listen to the rain, only the rain, and nothing else. No guns, no boat, no Bill…and finally I dozed off.

THE KEYS

When we stepped outside, the hot, moist air engulfed my body. Everywhere you looked it was green, and steam rose from the black top. It was ten o'clock, and people were busy going about their business. We got in the Ford and pulled out on the highway. After a few hours, Steve spotted a sign and read it out loud, "Key Largo." He asked Frank what a key was and Frank told him it was a small reef or island. The blue-green water sparkled on each side of the highway. I was glad when Frank pulled off the road and up to a cafe; I was starving. It looked like an old train caboose, only it was made of wood and tin. A sign on top of the roof read: Seven Mile Bridge Cafe. It was open from one end to the other on the front side, with a long wooden counter top that was coated in a shiny resin. It had about ten chrome swivel stools with red Naugahyde seat covers. It was crowded, and there were only two empty spots. Frank took one and I let Steve have the other. He plopped down in the stool and spun it around, banging his leg into a big, burly guy sitting next to him. The guy looked at Steve, and I thought for sure there was gonna be trouble, but Steve said, "Sorry," and the guy stood up, took a last drink of his coffee, and said, "No problem." Then looked at me, pointed to his seat, and said, "There ya go, buddy," and walked away. It just goes to show you, not everybody is an asshole and ya gotta stay positive, because you never know how a person is gonna react. I jumped on the stool and spun around once before facing the small kitchen area. And then I was face-to-face with a pretty, young waitress with bright red lipstick and blonde hair pulled back in a ponytail with a big yellow bow in it. She greeted us with a big smile and said, "How can I help ya?" She was wearing a white tight-fitting dress with a pink apron over it. The apron had Seven Mile Bridge Cafe written on it in sparkly silver letters. Her name tag said "Cat." Frank ordered pancakes and two eggs. Steve and I got the thick French toast because Cat told us "it was to die for." The cook was a dark-skinned, wiry guy with coal-black hair. He looked over at us a few times and smiled. I noticed he had a couple of teeth missing and figured he was an ex-con gone straight. He might have been an ex-preacher for all I know. But if I had to bet money, I'd say ex-con.

He cracked eggs on the side of the stove with one hand, and they crackled as they spilled out on the hot grill. At the same time as he was making the eggs, he poured the pancake batter into three perfect circles. Then he dunked the thick French bread into a bowl filled with a secret French toast mixture and plopped them next to the pancakes. This guy was a pro, a real artist, and his moves were quick and precise with no wasted energy. You could tell he took great pride in what he did. It made me want to be a cook. Steve and I spun around in the chairs looking at the surrounding area. It was beautiful, and everywhere you looked there was water. I could see living here, learning how to cook, and working in a place like this. Frank never spun his chair; he really didn't know how to have fun. Cat brought our food over to us, and she was right; it was some tasty French toast. The crust was a little crispy, and there was powdered sugar sprinkled over it all, and whatever his secret mixture was, you couldn't get the next bite into your mouth quick enough. I wondered if he was a cook on the inside, because if he was, I bet he got special treatment. Cat was real friendly and told us the Seven Mile Bridge was really cool, but a little scary, especially when it was rainy and stormy, but we shouldn't be bothered about that because there were no storms or rain forecast and apologized for even bringing it up. She told us she lived on Key Largo with her Nana and had a three-year-old daughter and that her boyfriend left when she was four months pregnant and that she had got real down for a while and even thought of killing herself. But she thought of her baby in her belly, and that's when she decided to name it Free. Because she was gonna make sure her baby was free of worries. She could really talk, and I don't think Steve or I got one word in other than "thanks" when we got up to leave. I hoped her dreams for her little girl would come true, but I didn't see how that was possible because she already had one giant strike against her by not having a dad.

The drive across the Seven Mile Bridge was mind boggling. It stretched out for as far as you could see, and it wasn't very high off the water at all. The ocean was a clear blue-green and in places you could see the bottom. How the hell did they manage to build it? How do you dig holes in the sand? Have you ever tried to dig a hole at the beach and a wave comes up and water rushes in and it collapses in on itself? It can't be done. I couldn't imagine how they did it. When I stopped thinking about the bridge, I started to feel bad, tired—even afraid for some reason. The bridge finally ended and we hit Sunshine Key. We stopped for gas and a piss, then drove over a bunch of narrower bridges till we reached Boca Chica where a jet blew over the top of the car so low we all howled at the sound. We pulled over, got out of the car, and watched jets roar over the highway and land at the air base. Every time one would cross over head, the whole bridge would move. I would tilt my head back and wait. First I would hear the distant hum, then in an instant it was on me, a deafening roar and a black flash smudging the glare of the sun for an instant. It shook my body from head to toe, and I screamed every time. One time I tried to hold in the scream, but my body was so filled up with energy that it burst out on its own. I could have stayed there for hours, but Frank and Steve got bored and wanted to go. When we got back in the Ford, my ears were still ringing and my body was tingling. We finally reached Key West, which was marked by a color-ful sign that said: Welcome to Key West, Paradise, USA. It was a beautiful sign with a bright orange sunset over an emerald bay, and a palm tree bending over it with red and yellow flowers, and a conch shell sitting on a sandy white beach. It really did look like paradise. The sign next to it was the diamond-shaped Mile Marker Zero.

Zero, it left me with a strange feeling in my gut. On our way down, we had noticed a lot of military trucks and jeeps coming and going on the road. Key West was their destination. There were young sailors with short haircuts everywhere. Most of them wore baggy-leg white pants that were tight at the waist and white T-shirts with a pack of cigs rolled up in the sleeve, and they topped it off with a white sailor cap. The cap is how they showed their personality. Some tilted them to the left, others to the right, some wore them low in front, right down to their eyebrows, others at the back of the head. I thought they looked cool. I especially liked the hat and thought maybe one of them would trade me for my cowboy hat. We got a pizza to go from a little Italian joint and drove out a deserted road and parked under a palm tree. We sat on some rocks not far from the water's edge and dug in. It was a decent pizza and we finished it off quick. We each got three slices. We sat there for a long time not knowing what to do next. Steve and I tossed rocks into the water for a while, then we spotted a coconut in a tree and managed to knock it down. We tried to peel off the brown husk. We knocked it with a rock and threw it on the ground, but that sucker wasn't coming off. We spent at least an hour working at it, but it was no use. We went back over to where Frank was sitting and sat there for a while before Frank said, "We need guns and ammunition." He told us he had spotted an Army Navy surplus store in town and we should go check it out. I agreed, but I told him that first we should bury our wallets with our ID, so if we got caught, they wouldn't know who we were. Both Frank and Steve agreed. I'm not sure how I came up with this idea, other than I never wanted to go back home, no matter what.

We left the Ford a couple of blocks down the street just to play it safe. We browsed through the store looking at all the cool guns and knives. A guy behind the counter asked if he could help, but I said, "Nah." Then Steve asked if he could see a foot-long Bowie knife inside a glass case. The guy reached under the glass countertop and set it on a wooden plank so Steve could look at it. He picked it up, felt its weight, looked closely at its handle and said to the guy, "Nice, really nice. What's the price on it?" Frank was watching Steve, and Frank had an irritated look on his face. The guy said, "I'll give it to you for eight bucks." I was worried Steve was gonna do something stupid, like bolt out the front door with it, so I put my hand on his arm and said, "Let's go get an ice cream." He looked at me, smiled, and said, "Oh yeah."

He dropped the big knife on the board and I said thanks to the guy. Then Frank did a weird thing—he said, "I'll take it." He walked over and dropped eight bucks on the table. The guy put the big knife in a leather sheath and handed it to Frank. Frank undid his buckle, slipped his belt through the sheath loop, and let it hang on his hip. It looked real cool. Frank strutted out the front door and we followed. From the crybaby look Steve had on his face, I could tell he was jealous that Frank got the knife. So, I said, "Hey, let's go get some soft serve." Frank said, "Sure." You could tell he was in a cocky mood the way he strutted down the street with that big ass Bowie knife strapped to his hip. We headed down the street to the ice cream place. Steve kept looking at the knife on Frank's hip, and when we got to the soft serve ice cream place, he ordered the biggest one he could get, dipped in chocolate, just to piss Frank off. But I don't think Frank even cared. He had something on his mind. We sat at a table out front and licked the cones like crazy. It was warm, so they were dripping faster than you could lick. You had to hold it away from you so it wouldn't get all over you. Steve was a mess; the giant soft serve was too much for him to handle. He got it on his chin, his shirt, his pants. And just as a big fuckin' drip plopped on his shoe, I screamed, "Holy shit!" I couldn't fuckin' believe what a mess he was, but he didn't seem to care. He was just Steve. Frank watched him and shook his head. Frank had very neat eating habits, and Steve almost always pissed him off a little, but this mess was beyond anything either of us had ever witnessed. Besides, Frank was in one of his moods and didn't talk for hours. None of us did. I think the idea of breaking into that place was on our minds, and then there was the boat.

We walked around town for a bit, then made our way to the street behind the Army Navy store and saw that it was a cement block building with a low, flat roof. A metal ladder was attached to the side of the building for roof access, and there were no lights in the small gravel parking lot. Frank had to tell Steve not to stare two different times, and when Steve asked why, Frank told him to shut the fuck up. Later, I explained to Steve about not acting conspicuous. He didn't know what that word meant exactly, so I had to explain it to him. He understood and apologized to Frank. We walked down by the boats and spotted a pretty good size fishing boat and figured it would hold at least a hundred guys. We all agreed it was better than nothing. My mind kept imagining holding a gun on the captain, but I couldn't quite work that thought all the way through. I decided to focus on breaking into the Army Navy store. All the windows and doors had bars on them, so going through the roof was our best option. I could imagine digging through the tar and then through to wood, making a hole big enough for one of us to slide through, then passing guns and ammo up to the others. One to keep watch, the other to grab the stuff from the guy below. That made sense to me; it seemed realistic. But the boat...that was a whole different thing. We banged around town for hours, and Frank had a prostitute ask him if he was horny and if he was looking for a good time. He just walked past her, but Steve was interested in her and how much she would charge. She had lots of long hair that hung down her back, and she wore high heels and a loose dress that moved softly between her long legs when the wind blew. The buttons were open halfway down her chest. You would never guess she was a prostitute. She was pretty and sexy as hell. I gotta say, I was curious about the cost too, because if I had the money I would have taken her up on her offer. I wondered why people had such a big problem with prostitution and made it illegal. If I was old enough to vote, I would vote to legalize it because she made me horny, and the idea of getting thrown in jail for having sex with her made me mad as hell. With my luck, I probably would get caught.

We walked along the water's edge and ended up standing in front of a giant landmark in the shape of a buoy. It had to be fifteen feet tall. It was painted red, black, and yellow, with white lines separating each color. In bold letters it read: SOUTHERN MOST POINT CONTINENTAL U.S.A. But the most import thing it said was: Ninety Miles to Cuba. The top had a triangle shape outlined in yellow, with a turquoise center, and a conch shell right in the middle. We stood there for a long time and stared at it. Ninety miles, ninety miles, I kept repeating over and over in my head. Stop, just focus on the guns and ammo for now: keep it simple.

It was 3:00 a.m. and the streets were dead. We pulled the Ford into the parking lot behind the Army Navy surplus store and shut the lights off. It was dark and quiet as a tomb, and we could hear each other breathe. Frank said, "Let's do it." As we walked toward the building, the crunch of gravel under our feet seemed insanely loud. When we reached the building, we stood still and listened. Nothing. We climbed the rusted metal ladder up to the roof. My heart was racing. I'm not sure what Frank or Steve was thinking; none of us talked.

We had a crowbar and the Bowie knife. Steve kept watch as planned, and I dug first. The knife was sharp as hell, but the tar was thick and hard. When I got tired, Frank went at it. It was much harder and slower work than we had imagined. I was sweating, and we had barely made a two-inch hole through which we could see down into the store. We kept our focus and complained in whispers to each other about what a fucker it was. I was watching Frank dig when I caught sight of a set of headlights pulling up next to the Ford. Steve didn't even see it because he was watching us. I grabbed Frank's hand and said, "Car," in a whisper. We all flattened on the roof. There was nowhere to go. We just had to wait. We heard the ladder move; someone was coming up. Then a flashlight shined on us. A voice said, "Stay down. Put your hands out in front of you." I glanced up and saw a cop. We followed orders. I felt numb, exhausted, afraid. Then I heard the cop holler, "Come on up." When the second cop reached the rooftop, the first one said to him, "We got some pros here," and then he laughed. The second cop told us to put our hands behind our backs and he handcuffed us. The edges of the cuffs hurt my wrists, and I couldn't get them to feel comfortable, but I didn't say anything. They told us to stand, which is no easy feat when your hands are cuffed behind your back. They led us over to the ladder and helped us climb to the ground, but they never took the cuffs off. I was afraid I was gonna fall and my mouth was dry. They put us in the patrol car and took us to the police station.

They sat me in a hard wooden chair in front of an empty desk. I didn't know what they had done with Frank and Steve, but I figured they were gonna talk to us separately. The room was small and in need of paint. There were two long-tube fluorescent lights above the desk; one was out. A dirty corkboard hung on the wall with photos of some rough looking guys on it. The desk had a clutter of papers and a big ashtray filled with cigar butts that gave the room a rancid smell. A big tan leather chair stared at me from across the desk; it looked new and out of place. The cop who had handcuffed me walked in with a big, dark-skinned guy who, from where I was seated, looked about seven feet tall and must have weighed three hundred pounds. He had a clipboard in one hand, which he was looking at, and a cup of coffee in the other. He took a slug of coffee and set it down on the desk, then dropped down into the big leather chair. The coffee was so strong I could smell it from where I was sitting. That, along with the rotten cigar smell, made me want to puke. He was wearing a sloppy white shirt with sweat stains under the arms. He hadn't shaved for a few days, and his mustache ran down past the corners of his mouth. He reminded me of one of the sleazy Mexican bad guys in the movie *The Treasure of the Sierra Madre*. No doubt about it, he was a scary fucker. The other cop stood by the door with his arms folded across his chest and a shit-eating grin on his face. Without looking up, the big cop casually asked me my name. I didn't answer. He looked up from the paper, stared at me, and asked again, "What's your name?" I'll be damned if he didn't have a Mexican accent. My mouth was dry, and I could feel my face doing weird shit. I said, "I'm sorry, but I'm not gonna tell you my name." It sounded stupid and weak, but I said it again. "I'm not gonna tell you." His face swelled up, his eyes bulged, and he jumped to his feet and leaned across the desk so that his face was only inches from mine. I could smell his rancid cigar and coffee breath. This time he spit the words, "What the fuck is your name? And I'm not gonna ask again!" My mouth twisted downward, I felt like I couldn't breathe, but I said it again. "I'm sorry, sir, but I'm not gonna tell you." He hovered over me for a moment, and I thought he was gonna bash me in the face, but then he dropped back down in his chair and said to the other cop, "Get this idiot out of here." The smiley cop took me by the arm and led me out the door. I wanted to yell, "Fuck you, I'm no idiot," and "We don't need no stinking badges." But I didn't. He walked me down a narrow hallway and up some stairs to an empty cell. Then he unlocked the door, took the handcuffs off, gave me a little shove inside, and shut the squealing iron door behind me.

The room was a small square with a bunk bed, a toilet, a sink, a shower, and a small table with two bench seats. Everything was metal and built right into the floor, and it was all grey, including the walls, ceiling, and floor. There were bars that ran from wall to wall behind the table, and a brick wall about three feet behind that, with a small window with bars. I sat down on the lower bunk and breathed a sigh of relief. I did it. I didn't tell that ugly bastard my name. I wondered if Frank and Steve would stick to our plan and not tell their names. I heard the sound of a trash truck through the small window and looked up at it. The dim glow of the morning light penetrated the darkness, and I had an empty feeling in my gut. I wondered when they would serve breakfast or if they would starve me till I told them my name. I walked over to the metal sink and turned the water on. I stuck my mouth under the faucet and gulped some water. It tasted okay. I don't know what I expected, maybe a metal taste from rusted pipes or something. I looked at the toilet; it didn't have a lid or seat, just a metal bowl to sit your ass on. I wouldn't have to worry about putting the seat down, something I was always guilty of forgetting and then having my mom yell at me. I wondered how my little brother was doing. I felt bad for leaving him. He would like the top bunk. It's funny when you're alone how the mind fantasizes shit, like this was our room, not a jail, and I worked at a burger joint in town sweeping up and doing dishes, and he would go to the local school. I wouldn't make a lot of money, but we could eat all we wanted, because that was one of the perks of the job.

The sound of keys rattled outside the door. It swung outward and Steve walked in. The heavy metal door squealed shut behind him. He stood there for a moment, looked around, and then said, "I got the top bunk." I smiled and said, "Sure." He recounted all the shit that went down with him and the big, ugly bastard, and he told me he was scared shitless, but didn't give him his name. He told me he heard them say that because Frank was eighteen he was going into the regular jail. He said he thought it was called the bullpen or something like that. I told Steve a bullpen is where they keep the guys all together in a big room. I had learned a few jail terms from my dad. We agreed that our cell wasn't that bad. After a while, we heard a rattling at the door and a small opening with a six-inch shelf swung in and a turnkey said, "Breakfast." He passed in a metal tray with a metal plate with two pancakes, two sausages, some eggs, and a cup of coffee. Steve grabbed it, then the guy passed another one through. I got a quick glance at the guy's face. He looked worn, like a repeat offender. I said, "Thanks," and the small opening shut. When I sat down at the table, Steve had already poured the tin of syrup onto his pancakes and was taking his first bite. "Good," he mumbled. I poured the syrup onto mine and took a bite. It tasted horrible. I thought maybe it was the syrup, so I took a bite of a piece I hadn't gotten any syrup on yet, but it was still shit. I mean it was so bad I couldn't eat it. I tried a couple of more bites, but finally gave up and slid them onto Steve's plate. I ate the sausages. They were bad, but I could at least get them down. Eggs are eggs. Then I took a swig of coffee. It was thick and black in the metal cup, and so damn strong and bitter I almost spit it out. I wasn't used to drinking it without milk, but you would have had to pour a gallon of milk in that shit to cut the bitter taste. Steve ate everything and had a content look on his face. I was still hungry.

The next four days went by slow. Nothing much happened. The food was generally shit. We got oatmeal for breakfast one morning, with a little tin of brown sugar, raisins, and milk. I gotta say, it was better than the oatmeal at the Salvation Army, but not by much. Steve got on a kick about buying a '57 Ford Thunderbird when he got out. He asked if I thought moon hubcaps would look good. He wanted black paint with a red interior. He told me he would probably get an automatic because he didn't like shifting. I remembered his turn at driving and grinding the gears and thought, no shit. We were bored to death, and I was getting sick of him repeating the story of his dream T-bird. Late one afternoon, while we were staring at each other, we decided to take Steve's watch apart and make a checker board. It had a metal band, and we popped the little pieces off and set them on the table. When we got our dinner that night, it was some weird meat, mashed potatoes, gravy, and a little broccoli. I tested the gravy. It tasted like burnt grease, so I gave it to Steve. I finally wised up and instead of just giving him stuff, I would trade him for something I liked. He usually got the better end of the deal, because if he didn't want to trade he would just say, "Nope," and I would end up giving him the shit I didn't like anyway. During dinner, we used one of the forks to scrape a checker board on the top of the table, and after we finished our shit food we played our first game. Steve was good at it. He beat me every game. He didn't say shit, but I hated the smile on his face after he would beat me. I finally had enough and told him I was tired and got in my bunk, but I couldn't sleep. I kept thinking how I was gonna beat him if it took me twenty years. I wondered how long we were gonna be in here, because I was so tired of him talking about his dream T-bird and watching him eat with his mouth open and making animal noises that I wanted to kill myself. He climbed up into his bunk and said, "Night." I said, "Night," back. I wanted to say fuck you and your stupid T-bird and why don't you eat with your mouth closed and stop all the other shit that you do to irritate me, but I didn't. I just lay there. I felt closed in. I remember my dad telling me jail wasn't that bad. He was wrong; I hated it. I wanted out. I wanted to see the sun, and even though I didn't want to, I started to cry. I kept it all to myself; I didn't want the asshole above me to hear. His bunk started to shake a little and I knew Steve was jerkin' off. I was halfway playing with my own dick when I started to think of Suzi White and her red pubic hair.

It was still dark outside when the sound of a cell door opening and voices woke me up. I got out of my bunk and listened at the door. I heard a guy say, "I'm hungry, when do we git somethin' ta eat?" The other voice said, "When you get it," in a rough, angry tone. The door slammed shut, and I could hear the guy in the cell saying, "I don't know why I'm here. I didn't do anything wrong." I lay back down in my bunk and fell back to sleep, thinking, I didn't do anything wrong, that's bullshit.

I woke up to the sound of the cubby door opening, and sure enough, like clockwork, so did Steve. He made his irritating morning noises, and I realized I was still pissed at him. I went and grabbed my tray and sat at the table. I was hoping he would oversleep because I was gonna eat all my pancakes just to piss him off, even though they tasted like shit. He sat down with his tray across from me and gave me one of his sausages and half his eggs. I slid the poison pancakes onto his plate, along with the syrup. When we heard voices in the hall, he looked up. I liked having the upper hand and told him they'd brought a new guy in last night. He asked who he was. I told him I didn't know but that I heard him say he didn't know why he was here and that he didn't do anything wrong. Steve said, "That's what all criminals say," and I guess he was right. I knew we were guilty. The cubby closed and we heard the guy say, "When do I git out? I didn't do anythin' wrong." He had a Southern accent. I got up and went to the door. I wanted somebody, anybody, to talk to other than Steve. I said, "Hey, what's your name?" There was a brief pause, then the voice said, "Carney, my name is Carney." "I'm Chip. Nice to meet you." He said, "I don't like the pancakes, but I'm hungry so I ate 'em." I said, "Yeah, they suck." Steve hollered, "I like them," and told him his name was Steve. "What did you boys do to git yourself in here?" he asked. I told him our story, and he said it didn't sound fair cause we were just tryin' ta help some guys and that they should give us a medal or somethin'. I laughed and told him that wasn't gonna happen, and then I asked him what he was in for. He went into an elaborate story about this underage girl who they said he had sex with and he didn't remember any of it because he was drinking and didn't even know who she was. It didn't sound right to me. I could tell he was guilty, but I didn't say that. I just said, "Sure," and let it go. Over the next week, we got to know Carney a little, and he would sneak us cigarettes and matches in the broom that we got every few days to sweep our cell with. He would get the broom first, stick a couple of cigs in it, and pass it over to us. It made us all feel like we were putting something over on the turnkey, whose name was Willy, and wasn't a bad guy, other than he said we couldn't have cigs because we were underage. He did bring us some sleazy sex books to read though, which increased our jerkin' off by about 50 percent. The days rolled on, and I got tired of listening to Carney complain about being in jail for something he didn't think he did. I realized he had a way of thinking about things that wasn't real. He had Steve convinced we were heroes and that they should let us go and give us a medal. I knew it was bullshit. The more I thought about what we had done, the more I realized it was all bullshit. None of us were happy at home and we just wanted out. We were just running away, that's all. I knew Steve was just going along, following Frank and me, but I didn't know what Frank was thinking because I hadn't seen or heard from him since the night we got caught. I knew if I ever got out of jail, I wasn't going back home. I figured I could go back to Rosie's place and do odd jobs for her, and when I had breaks I could lie on the beach and take a swim whenever I got too hot. I thought about those grits and shrimp. I would taste each and every one of those sauces and maybe even help Rosie make up a new sauce.

We counted twenty-two days since we got put in jail, and I was beginning to hate it a lot. The only good thing was that at night, through our cell window, we could hear the music at the USO building just outside. Willy told us that USO stood for United Service Organization and that it was a place where they played live music for members of the United States Armed Forces and their families. "Twistin'" by Chubby Checker played all the time, and we would even dance to it every once in a while. "The Lion Sleeps Tonight" came on, and I sang along. Steve joined in, and I think we sounded pretty good, because Carney commented on it. He said he didn't sing but he thought we both had good voices. Steve got on a kick about us starting up a band. I thought that a band was a good idea, but when I got out, the last thing I wanted to do was hang out with him. He was just so fucking boring. But at least he had something to talk about other than that '57 T-bird. I thought that when I got out, if I even saw one on the street, I would puke. I tried really hard not to be an asshole, but every once in a while, when he would get on the T-bird kick, I would just get in my bunk and turn my back on him. The problem was, the fucker kept on talking. Finally one afternoon, when he was ranting on about the black metallic paint for about the billionth time, I said, "You're not gonna get a T-bird. You don't have any money, you don't even have an idea for a job, and we might not get out of jail for ten years, and by then they would be junk." He just stared at me for a long time and didn't say anything. I felt like shit, but I wasn't going to apologize, because if I did, I knew he would go right back to talking about it. So I just sat there and stared right back at him. The sound of a key unlocking our door broke our standoff.

JUDGEMENT DAY

A burly cop stood at the door and told us to step out. We were going to see the judge. He put handcuffs on us and walked us down the hall to the steps, then down to the lower floor and out a metal door into the sunlight. The sun felt so good on my face. I stopped for a moment and closed my eyes. "Move it," the burly cop said. We walked by an old tree in the courtyard, and he told us it was called "the hangin' tree" because in 1888 they hung some poor son of a bitch from it. I didn't know if he was bullshitting and just trying to scare us, or if it was true, but why would anybody make up a story like that? He walked us across the street to the courthouse. People stared at us and it made me feel like shit. I don't know why he had to handcuff us, I wasn't gonna run anywhere. Or maybe I would. I guess they didn't want to chance it. We walked up the stairs and he led us into the courthouse and down a long corridor lined with people, some sitting in chairs and some just milling around.

They all looked miserable, and one woman was even crying over something the guy talking to her was saying. The cop opened the door to the courtroom and we walked in. It wasn't a big courtroom like I expected; it was just a room with a long table in it. Frank was seated on the right side of the table, and the cop sat me and Steve next to him. I didn't know if we were supposed to talk, but I said, "Hey, Frank, you okay?" He said, "Yeah," and then the cop told us to shut it. A few minutes later, a large woman came in wearing a long black judge's robe. The cop told us to stand, so we did, then he announced her name, "The Honorable Judge Rousek." I didn't know they had women judges, but I could tell right away she was serious and not somebody to be messed with. She had a big forehead and grey hair pulled back tight off her face. I didn't know why, but the idea that she was a commie bastard came to mind. She called each of us by our names and told us that what we were attempting was foolish, and that even the military made a mess of the Bay of Pigs, and they were supposedly trained professionals. She explained that the store owner wasn't going to press charges, and that Frank's stepdad was going to pay to have it repaired, and that he was flying down in a few days and would drive us all back home.

She recommended that Steve and I join the armed services as soon as we turned seventeen and maybe go in on the buddy plan because, with our family histories, it would probably help us get on the right path. She was looking right at me when she was talking, and I was looking right at her. She had dark empty eyes, with dark circles under them. She reminded me of Steve's mom, except for the nose. I wondered if she had big tits under her black robe. She scared me, she made me feel foolish and young. I don't know why she picked me to stare at. Then she said, "Do you understand what I'm saying, young man?" I said, "Yes, ma'am." I'll never forget her final words. "The good lord gave us free will, it's up to us to make good choices. That will be all." The cop led us out of the courthouse and into the street. The sun felt good on my face, but my mind was racing. How did they find out our names? It had to be Frank. Steve had never left my sight, unless he told them that first night. Then I thought of the buddy system. No way! I didn't really hate Steve, but I wanted to be away from him for a while. We walked past the hangin' tree, and I wondered what the guy did to get hung. One thing for sure, he didn't make good choices.

FED UP

When we got inside the jail, the cop turned us over to Willy, who led us up the stairs to our cell. He opened the door to our little box, and Steve and I stepped inside. It seemed horribly small, smaller than an hour ago when we took our walk to see the judge. I wondered how many days it would be before Frank's stepdad got here. I was hoping Steve wouldn't talk, but no such luck. He started in about the T-bird. I listened for about ten seconds, then I started screaming at him to shut the fuck up. He told me to shut the fuck up, and then he punched me in the face and knocked me backward into the shower. I got up and started swinging wildly and he was swinging back. We wrestled to the floor, swinging, kicking, and yelling at each other. Then the son of a bitch bit me on my shoulder. I screamed in pain and pinned his head between the toilet and the shower and punched him in the face. Willy pounded on the door and yelled, "Knock it off or I'm gonna call the guard." Gasping for air, I pushed myself away from Steve and fell back against the bunk, exhausted. I looked at his ugly teeth marks in my shoulder and wanted to bash him in the face again. I couldn't believe that crazy bastard punched me in the face and bit me. I looked over at him as he wiped blood from his nose. I hated his stupid ass, and I'm sure he hated me. But then he said something ridiculous. He said, "You're just jealous because I'm gonna have a cooler car than you." I fucking started laughing like hell and so did he. We hugged each other and said, "Sorry." Then we both started crying. You would think jail would make you tougher, not turn you into a big fucking crybaby.

They took Carney away that afternoon. He had told us earlier they had evidence against him and that he was guilty of rape. I liked Carney, but I didn't feel bad for him. Willy had told us on the down low that the girl was only twelve. I didn't know how long he was gonna be in jail, but one thing you do have in jail is time to think. I hoped he would realize that what he did was wrong.

That night we got steak, potatoes and gravy, carrots, and a piece of key lime pie. It was all shit, but I ate every bit of it. It was Friday night and the USO was hopping. Chubby was doing his thing singing, "Twistin' the Night Away." Steve got up and started to dance, but I wasn't in the mood. I lay on my bunk and watched him gyrate. He was a still a spaz, but a decent dancer, and watching him made me smile, even though I didn't want to. I was thinking about getting out and going home. I wanted out, but I didn't want to go home to that miserable apartment. I wondered how my little brother was. But then I remembered my dad would be there, and I didn't want to face him. I also wondered what my mom would say. I decided that when I got back, or maybe even before, I would take off. Steve mentioned going into the navy on the buddy plan and saving money to buy his T-bird. I said, "Sure," because I didn't want to get in another fight, and I didn't want to make him feel bad, but I definitely wasn't doing that. The idea of some asshole pulling your bunk apart because it wasn't made just right and yelling at you telling you what a little cockroach you were didn't appeal to me. I had no idea if that's how it really was, but from what I had seen in movies, no thank you. The problem was, no matter how hard I tried to think about what I was gonna do, I couldn't come up with anything. I lay there and listened to music for a while and then a slow song came on, "The Great Pretender" by the Platters. I imagined sailors dancing with their girlfriends and wives and felt real lonely.

I slept solid that night and didn't hear Willy bring breakfast. When I woke up, Steve was at the table eating and said, "Morning." I got up and stumbled to the table. He looked bad. He had two black eyes and his nose was all swollen. I felt bad for what I had done, till I looked at where he bit me. It was all swollen and black and blue. I wondered if I needed a tetanus shot or if that was only for animal bites. I took a sip of the black mud they called Cuban coffee and ate my eggs and sausages. I was actually getting used to the coffee and looked forward to my first sip in the morning.

It seemed quiet. I couldn't hear much street noise and remembered it was Saturday and that's how it was in the early morning. Things didn't get hopping till around ten. We spent the day lazing around as usual, wondering if Frank's stepdad was gonna show. The day passed like every day in jail—thinking about the outside and making the best of being stuck inside a little box. We played about twenty games of checkers, but by this time we knew each other's moves so well that whoever was more bored or distracted usually lost. It could go either way. We didn't talk about going home.

TO BE OR NOT TO BE

The next morning, right after breakfast, Willy came to the door and opened it. He said, "Okay, my two gangsta friends, it's time to go home to mama." As he walked us down the hall, he stopped abruptly and turned to face us. He said, "So what did you learn?" I couldn't tell if he was fuckin' with us or wanted a serious answer. Steve said, "Don't get caught next time." Willy said in a real serious voice, "Don't be a dumbass." Then he looked at me and said, "So?" I didn't want to piss him off, and the only thing I could think was, "Make good choices." I didn't know what that meant, but it seemed to be the right answer because he nodded. We walked down the stairs and out the front door into the sunshine. Frank and his stepdad where standing there waiting for us. Standing next to his stepdad, Frank looked small and frail. It was awkward as hell. Steve and I nodded at Frank, and he nodded back, but we didn't say a word. Glen, that was Frank's stepdad's name said, "Well, let's get going. We have a long way to go." I couldn't take my eyes off Frank. He looked whiter than normal and miserable, and I wondered what he and his stepdad had talked about. We got into the Ford, which was parked at the curb. Frank got in front, Steve and I in the back. It all felt bad. I wanted to run away, but I didn't. We drove through town and passed by the soft serve ice cream place. I wanted one so bad, but knew better than to say anything. Then Steve said, "Excuse me, Glen, do you think we could stop and get a soft serve?" I was shocked that Steve even opened his mouth, but it was one time I was glad he did. Glen said, in a dead sorta voice, "Not today." Not today? When I thought? I didn't like Glen. There was something about him that made it hard for me to breathe. I stared out the window at the palm trees and spotted a coconut stuck up in the top of one and thought of how Steve and I tried to crack that one open for hours. We drove for a while and it was deathly quiet. Glen pulled into a gas station and we all got out to piss. Steve went first, then Glen. I waited at the door for him to come out. He looked at me with disgust as I went in. Fuck that guy. I went into the dingy bathroom and took a piss, and while I was standing over the shit-splattered toilet bowl looking down at it, I thought, that's life. When I walked out, Frank was standing there waiting. We made eye contact for a second. I smiled at him and he smiled at me, but we didn't say anything. Then he went into the bathroom. I walked back to the car thinking about running but figured there would be a better opportunity, so I didn't. Steve was sitting in the back seat and Glen was at the wheel. The car was running. We waited. Glen said, "Where's Frank?" I didn't want to answer him because he knew he was takin' a piss and was just irritated he had to wait for him. He asked again, and I shot back, "Takin' a piss." We waited a few more minutes, and he told me to go tell him to hurry up, that the car was running. I got out, and as I walked to the bathroom I thought of saying, "Hey, Frank, the car is running!" What a stupid thing to say. I got to the bathroom door and said, "Hey, Frank, did something die in there?" It was a dumb joke we had when one of us would take a nasty crap. He didn't answer, so I knocked and said, "Hey, Frank, are you in there?" No answer. I turned the handle, but it was locked, so I walked inside the little market and looked around, but he wasn't in there either. I thought, holy fuck, he took off. Why didn't he tell me? I would have gone with him. I looked all around the gas station and up the streets. I didn't see him anywhere. You fucker, where are you? I kept thinking, now is the time. Just run. Run just like Frank did. But I didn't. I walked back to the car and told Glen I couldn't find him. Glen shut the car off and said, "What do you mean you can't find him?" I wanted to say, "What the fuck do you think can't find him means?" But I didn't because I could tell by the angry-ass look on his face he was in no mood for back talk. He charged back over to the bathroom and I followed. He yanked on the door, pounded on it, and yelled, "Open the goddamn door, Frank." No answer. He went into the market, got an extra key, and strode back to the door and yanked it open—then fell back a little saying, "Oh my God." I stepped into the doorway and saw Frank hanging there from a chain hooked to the bar over the toilet bowl. I knew he had hooked the chain, stood on the toilet, and jumped off. His eyes were bulged out and his head had a blue color to it. His limp body just hung there. He was dead. I just stood there. Some guy pushed past me with Frank's stepdad and I watched as they struggled to get the chain unhooked and lower his body. I heard Steve's voice asking me what happened. What happened? I calmly said, "Frank hung himself."

Police cars, ambulances, and a crowd of looky-loos swarmed the gas station. I couldn't help but listen to the whispers in the crowd. "Why did he do it?" "God he was just a young kid." "Is he with God now, Mommy?" a little girl asked her mother. "No, honey," the mother replied. "God doesn't accept you if you hurt yourself." "He was probably on drugs," some guy in a suit said. I sat on a curb off to the side with Steve. I listened and watched. I felt numb to it all. Some woman, decked out in a nice suit and a neat hairdo, walked up to us with a microphone in her hand. A guy with a camera on his shoulder stood at her side. She spoke into the microphone and said, "Did you know the boy?" Then she held the microphone out in front of Steve. Steve said, "He was my friend." The woman got all excited, and her voice turned soft and sweet as she asked, "What happened?" I looked up at her dove eyes, and just as Steve said, "He hung himself," I yelled, "Fuck you, bitch whore," and I jumped up and started running down the street as fast as I could. I started screaming and crying. I ran and ran and ran till I found myself in a park. I ran behind some trees and dropped down on my knees and pounded the grass with my fists and cried till I ran out of tears and snot. I was mad at Frank. He'd left me alone, and I felt like I wasn't a good friend. We had a pact. I was a good friend, wasn't I? I thought he was a little crazy, but so was I. I'd thought of killing myself, but I didn't. I hurt, I had pain, fear, sadness. I guess he had more pain than I did to do what he did. I'm sorry, Frank, I'm sorry. A policeman walked up to me and knelt beside me. He said, "Are you okay, son?" I looked him right in the eyes and said, "Sure."

Frank's dad got us a hotel with adjoining rooms that night. He kept the door open so he could keep an eye on us in case we decided to run off, which didn't make sense because he fell asleep by ten o'clock. Steve and I had separate beds, and we just lay there for a long time in the dark. I kept waiting for him to say something about the fucking T-bird. I thought, thank God he's fallen asleep. Then he blurted out in a shaky voice, "Let's join the navy on the buddy plan. I can save up money and wait till I get out to buy—the you know what." Steve always made me laugh, no matter how bad I felt. But I didn't laugh that night. I thought of what Rosie had told me, "Don't drop the potato." I was trying like hell, but I was barely holding on to it.

I woke to the sound of Glen banging around in his room. It was still dark outside, but he had told us he wanted to get an early start in the morning. He stuck his head in our room and said, "Time to go." He had told us yesterday that he'd made all the arrangements to have

Frank's body shipped back to California and that he had talked to his wife and they'd decided to cremate him at a mortuary right here in town because it would be easier to ship the body that way. I don't know why he had to tell us all that shit, because it only made me feel worse than I already felt. I thought he was a mean fucker and was punishing us for being part of why Frank killed himself and why he was even down here in the first place. I didn't say anything back. But Steve asked if we were gonna get something to eat first because he was starving. Glen said, "Have you got any money?" Steve and I had used up all our money and Frank had been paying for everything. I didn't give a shit if I ate, even if I was starving. I didn't want that son of a bitch to buy my food. Steve said, "No, but my mom will pay you back when we get home." Glen laughed at that.

Right next door to the motel was a twenty-four-hour diner. I guess Glen was hungry because that's where we ended up. Steve ordered the special: three pancakes two eggs, two sausages, and a cup of coffee. Glen said, "All grown-up drinking coffee, huh?" I didn't order shit. Glen said, "Are you sure you're not hungry? I'm sure your dad will pay me back; I heard he was released from jail." I really hated his ass and thought, no wonder Frank killed himself. With a stepfather like you, I would too.

He drove for hours and didn't even stop for lunch, just filled his mug up with coffee. I was in the back seat passed out for hours. I asked Steve to ride up front because I couldn't stand sitting next to Glen and told him I might do something crazy like grab the steering wheel and drive us off a cliff, or head on into a semitruck. It was pitch black out when I opened my eyes, and I could see the back of Glen' s bald head. I didn't move an inch because I didn't want him to know I was awake and ask some dumb ask question like, are you hungry yet. I was starving, but I just shut my eyes and fell back to sleep.

I was lying there half-awake, when Glen turned off the highway and pulled up to a little cafe. "Anybody hungry?" Glen said in a smartass tone. Steve said, "Oh yeah," and we all walked into the restaurant. We took a seat in a booth, and an older waitress brought us three glasses of water. Steve and I gulped ours down. "Well now, you boys are thirsty," she said in a heavy Southern accent. "Do you all know what you're gonna have to eat?" Glen said, "I'll have the number two with coffee." I wanted to say, you are number two. Steve ordered his usual pancakes, sausage, and eggs over medium. When the waitress turned to me, I could feel Glen's eyes on me. I said, "Can I please have the eggs, grits, gravy, and biscuits, ma'am." I used the sweetest voice I had. She said, "That's number six and it comes with steak. How do you want your steak cooked?" I caught a glimpse of Glen's face, and his top lip was pulled tight like a snarling dog. "Well done, ma'am," I said, "and thank you." The waitress smiled and looked at Glen and said, "You certainly have raised some fine boys with real genuine manners." Glen nodded. He was biting down on his tongue hard, and I knew he wanted to kill me. I said, "Yes, ma'am, he's a good father." Then I looked at Steve and said, "Isn't he Steve?" Steve didn't know what the fuck I was doin', so he said, "Sure," and let it go at that. Then I said, "Oh, may I have a cup of coffee too." She looked at me and said, "Every once in a while is okay, you just don't want to get in the habit; they say it will stunt your growth." "Yes, ma'am," I said, and she walked away. I ate everything on my plate and so did Steve. Glen's omelet was runny in the middle so he had to send it back, and when the waitress brought it back he complained it was overdone. He ate his toast and drank his coffee, and when the bill came he told her he didn't want to pay for the omelet because he didn't eat it. I could tell the waitress didn't like the fact that he wasn't gonna pay for it, but she ended up taking it off the bill. To top it off, Glen didn't leave a tip, and when we were walking out I heard her say, half under her breath, "You could learn some manners from your boys." When we got to the car, Glen got behind the wheel, Steve sat in front, and I got in back. Glen's arms were straight as boards as he gripped the steering wheel. He was twisting his hands around it and he was breathing heavily. I was watching him close, but I still didn't expect what came next. He whirled around and hit me in the face with the back of his hand, then turned back around and drove away. Steve was smashed up against his door, worried he might be next. I yelled up at Glen, "My dad's gonna kick your ass for hitting me." Glen turned around and looked at me with rage in his eyes, and I thought he was gonna belt me again, but he yelled back, "Your dad's nothin' but a jailbird, just like you, and if he even comes near me or my home, I'll have his ass thrown back in jail. You hear me, you little turd?" I didn't say anymore. I didn't want to get smacked again, and I knew it wouldn't make a difference. We drove straight through, except for one night when Glen pulled over and slept for a few hours. He only stopped at drive-through restaurants and bought us just enough food so we didn't starve. I wondered if he hit Frank. Frank never told us anything about that, but Frank never told us anything. He wouldn't tell us about his real dad, or the mental institution—nothing. He held shit in even more than I did. We pulled into Glendale late on the fourth night. Glen dropped me off first, and I was happy about that. I nodded to Steve, he nodded back, and Glen pulled away. I watched the taillights disappear down the dark, empty street. I stood there. Frank was dead. I don't know what I felt. Lost, alone, empty. I walked to the back of the driveway and glanced up at the apartment. It was dark. I squatted down in front of the garage and leaned my back against it. I took a cigarette out of my pocket and lit it. I took a big drag and it tasted like shit. I realized I didn't like smoking. I didn't like the taste of it, the smell of it, or how it made me feel. I did it because Frank did it, and Steve did it, and so did most of the kids at school. I flicked it down the driveway and watched the sparks shoot into the air as it bounced along the blacktop and rolled to a stop. I quit. I sat there and thought about Bahia de Cochinos, hitchhiking from Arizona, Steve's T-bird, my little brother, my mom...my dad...Frank. I was trying to decide if I was gonna go up the stairs to the apartment or not. What would I do if I didn't? Where would I go? What would I eat? I was tired, hungry, and lost. There has got to be more to life than this, I thought. Then I stood and started up the wooden stairs. As I climbed, a voice in my head said, "Lache pas la patate. Don't drop the potato." I had to smile.